RENEGADE ATLAS

J. N. Chaney

TABLE OF CONTENTS

For Ashley,

An annoying sister

And an amazing friend.

ONE

"OH, FUCK," I muttered, dropping my coffee as I stared out through the window of the medical facility on Paragon III. The steaming black liquid spattered all over my pants, making me hop back a step. "Shit! Shit!"

I swiped my fingers along my leg, annoyed by my clumsiness. After a quick second, I looked again at the spectacle unfolding in the hospital yard. There were two dropships—Sarkonian, judging by the gold and red colors it carried—unloading nearly twenty armed, exosuit-wearing soldiers.

I hadn't spent much time this close to Sarkonian space, so I'd only had the chance to see their military a handful of times, but every instance had told me everything I needed to know: avoid these sons-of-bitches at all costs.

"Sir, would you like me to prepare for departure?" asked the voice in my ear. It was Sigmond, my ship's artificial intelligence. "It would seem you're about to have unwanted company."

"That might be a good idea," I said.

"Very good, sir."

I turned and fled across the hall, leaving the puddle of coffee for someone else to bother with.

Nurses and patients crowded the rooms, trying to look out the windows at the small army about to storm their building. I wondered if this was normal for them, seeing a pack of soldiers unloading on their front lawn. This far out into the Deadlands, I wagered it just might be.

I rounded the hall and instantly spotted Freddie in the third doorway. We made eye contact at once, and I already knew what he was going to say. "Captain, what's going on?"

"Looks like the Sarkonian military," I said, as I approached. He stepped aside to let me through.

Octavia was awake, sitting up in the hospital bed. She'd been here for nearly two days and was doing much better now, thanks to the surgical team and the incubation chamber they had on hand. When I brought her in, the doctors had said it was unlikely she'd recover, but she proved them wrong on that. "Captain, do we need to leave?" she asked.

"I don't know yet."

Hitchens was beside her, holding a small bucket of ice. "Goodness! We can't move her yet. She needs her rest!"

I pulled Freddie inside the room and shut the door, heading straight to the window so I could close the curtains. "Rest ain't a luxury we can afford, Doc."

"Do we know why they're here?" asked Octavia.

A voice exploded over the hospital com before I could answer.

"Attention, Union fugitives!" it said, like thunder overhead. "We know you are here! Surrender yourselves now or we will use extreme force!"

I looked at Octavia. "Does that answer your question?"

"Damn," she said, trying to straighten herself. "So much for my vacation."

I grabbed the wheelchair from across the room, which the nurse had folded and squeezed between the closet and bathroom door, and flattened the seat with my palm. "No time for vacations when you're with me," I said, pushing it close to the bed.

I offered my arm and she took it, using me as leverage as she eased herself over. "You're right. Why rest when I can get shot again?" She landed in the chair with a soft thud.

I smirked, rolling her away from the bed. "That's the spirit."

We rushed out of the room and into the hall. I was in the lead, pushing Octavia's chair as we made our escape, everyone else behind me. "Where are we going?" asked Hitchens.

"The ship," I said, over my shoulder. "Where else?"

"How do you plan to get by the—" Two Sarkonian soldiers appeared at the end of the hall. "—guards?"

The armored men raised their weapons the second they saw us. "Move!" I barked, rushing into a side room.

Multiple gunshots fired through the corridor, forcing us to take cover in a room. As soon as I was inside, I pulled out my pistol and set my back to the wall, then returned fire, delivering three rounds. They missed, and the Sarkonians fired again, forcing me to take cover. "Siggy, tell Abigail we're gonna be a bit."

"I shall inform her of your delay, sir," said the A.I.

"Attention, fugitives!" called one of the soldiers. "Surrender now! You cannot escape this facility!"

I leaned in, peaking through the crack in the door, spotting one of them. There was just enough room in the crack to fit a bullet, I guessed.

I eased my pistol up to the slit, taking a second to aim, and then…

The frame of the wooden door exploded as the round left my gun, sending splinters into the air.

It struck the only visible soldier, ripping his jaw from his skull. He twisted where he stood, collapsing onto the floor.

In a heartbeat, I leapt into the hall, spotting the second man as he turned to look at his newly-deceased friend.

Before he could react, I pulled the trigger and fired two shots. One in the head, the other in the chest.

The poor bastard was dead before he had a chance to react.

Octavia rolled her chair out as soon as the body fell. "That was messy," she said as we started moving again.

"You'd prefer a softer touch next time?" I asked, grabbing the handles behind her chair.

"Stop a second!" she snapped as we neared the two bodies.

"What's wrong?" I asked.

Octavia pointed at one of the rifles. "Give it here, Jace."

I snagged the gun and tossed it to her.

She gripped the weapon with both hands. "I figure if you're pushing, you can't aim, so I might as well pick up the slack."

"Good thinking," I said, handing the second rifle to Freddie, who took it with some hesitation.

Right as we started to move, another set of Sarkonians entered through the end of the hall ahead of us. Octavia unloaded a three-round burst, clipping their armor, and managing to snag one in the neck.

I let go of the chair, retrieved my pistol, and fired a set of shots. A bullet buzzed by my head right as I hit the still-standing soldier in the head and chest. "Hot damn!" I snapped. My adrenaline was in full overdrive.

"Like I said," remarked Octavia.

I grinned. "Not bad for a cripple."

She gave me a look. "Careful, Captain, or you'll be next."

We kept moving, running as fast as the chair would allow, but stopped when we neared a set of doors to the outer lobby. Both had a glass pane at their center.

I motioned for the others to stay back. With a quick glance, I spotted six soldiers, each in pairs of two. "Looks like half their squad is out there."

"What do we do?" asked Freddie, a slight crack in his voice.

"What do you think?" I asked, looking back at him. "We're not sitting here like a bunch of invalids." I looked at Octavia. "No offense."

She scowled at me. "Give me a target and get out of the way."

"Someone's eager for some killing. Okay, Hitchens, you're on chair duty. When I go out there—"

"You mean you're running into that room?" asked Freddie.

"Yeah, and you're staying here."

"You can't do this by yourself, Captain," he cautioned.

"I'm not. If you'd actually listen to me, you'd know that," I said.

He gulped, then nodded.

"Do what I say and we'll all make it out of here. Now, Hitchens, I need you to push Octavia out so the door cracks and she can get a decent view. Don't push her all the way. Are you following?"

"I-Is that safe?"

Octavia took his hand in hers. "It's okay, Doctor. Please, do as he says."

Hitchens took a deep breathe. "All right, if you think it's a good idea, Octavia."

"And you, Freddie," I continued. "You're the rear guard. Don't let anyone snipe us in the ass. You hear me?"

"I'm not coming with you?" he asked.

"Someone has to watch our backs. That's you, kid. I swear to the gods, I ain't dying from a bullet in the ass, you hear me?"

He nodded. "I won't let you down, Captain."

I turned back and raised my pistol. "That's good, Freddie, 'cus this sure as shit ain't the end of my story."

Two

"Stop right—" My bullet cut through the Sarkonian soldier's neck before he could finish the sentence.

His partner turned to me as I ran to the other side of the room, passing between the remaining five soldiers. In a panic, he unloaded his rifle, shots trailing me as I moved, ripping through the wall and, to my delight, his own teammate.

Asshole didn't know what hit him.

I reached another set of doors, diving through them. They flapped open, slamming into the walls and swinging backwards, toward the gunfire.

I rolled on my back, aiming my pistol at the swinging doors, firing every time they opened.

With the Sarkonians' attention on me, Octavia came rolling into the room, rifle in hand, and opened fire.

The first one took a straight hit in the back. His chest exploded as the bullet ripped through him, bringing shards of bone into the open air. He fell flat on his face, instantly dead.

One of the soldiers came at me, propping the doors open and extending a barrel in my face. I did the same to him, but before either of us could unload a round into the other's skull, the woman in the wheelchair ended him.

Blood spattered out of his neck and onto my pants, and I quickly scrambled back. "Fuck!" I snapped.

The remaining soldiers turned their attention to Octavia, but Hitchens was already pulling her into the hall again. I took the opportunity to get on my feet again.

By my count, we still had two more to go.

"Walk away and we won't kill you!" I yelled, throwing my back to the wall, just behind the doors.

"W-We have reinforcements coming! Surrender now and you won't be—"

Two loud blasts interrupted the soldier before he could finish, followed by what sounded like bodies hitting the floor. I looked across the hall, but the others were still hiding. "What the fuck was that?" I asked.

"You can come out now!" called a familiar voice.

"Abigail?" I swung the door open and stepped out.

Abigail stood behind the two fresh corpses, a large rifle in her arms. "I thought you could use the assistance."

Freddie came running out of the hall. "Sister Abigail!"

Hitchens and Octavia were right behind him. "Goodness!" exclaimed the doctor, looking at all the bodies and the blood pooling around them. "It looks like a warzone!"

"It is," I told him, then turned back to Abigail. "Why aren't you in the ship? Where's Lex?"

"With me, sir," answered Sigmond, his voice filling my ear. "I've locked down *The Star* until you return, rest assured."

"I had this covered, you know," I told the former nun as I approached her.

"I'm sure you did," she answered. "But we're pressed for time and there's an army coming."

"An army?" asked Hitchens.

I nodded. "She's right. There's bound to be more ships on the way. We need to get off this rock, and fast."

"Understood," said Octavia.

We raced through the rest of the building, towards the fifth loading platform where *The Renegade Star* waited.

The airlock was sealed, but Siggy opened it right as we had the ship in view. "Awaiting orders, sir," he said, once we were onboard.

"Get us in orbit and activate the cloak," I said, making my way through to the cockpit.

I spotted Lex in the lounge. She was playing a game on the viewscreen. Some kind of educational thing with numbers. "Hello, Mr. Hughes!"

"Hey kid," I said as I ran by.

A moment later, I was strapped into my chair, staring out the front of my ship as the engines primed. *The Renegade Star* began to lift off the dock, hovering briefly before moving forward.

We ascended through the massive opening in the bay, angled toward the nearby clouds.

"Sir, I'm picking up movement near a slip gap point," said Sigmond.

"More Sarkonian ships?" I asked.

"On the contrary, sir, it appears to be—"

"Attention, Renegade vessel," interrupted a husky voice on the com. "This is General Marcus Brigham with the *UFS Galactic Dawn*, hailing the vessel identified as *The Renegade Star*. Respond now or you will be met with extreme force."

"Fuck you," I chimed back. "Siggy, cut the com and get us out of here."

"Right away, sir."

As we tore through the atmosphere of the planet, Sigmond activated a slipspace tunnel. *The Galactic Dawn* was moving towards us, but we'd be well on our way before it arrived.

"Entering slipspace," announced Sigmond, this time over the ship's com. "Please remain seated."

The black void of normal space quickly dissipated as we moved into the emerald vortex. Yellow sparks flashed along the tunnel walls as the rift closed behind us, separating us from our would-be pursuers.

"That's the second time that Brigham guy has found us," I said. "The Sarkonians must have sent a message before we escaped."

"That is very improbable, sir," said Sigmond.

"Oh? You got another theory?"

"The *UFS Galactic Dawn* arrived out of slipspace as we made our escape, not long after the Sarkonian dropship landed at the hospital."

"So?"

"Between the time the Sarkonians landed and the moment the Union ship emerged from the tunnel, only fourteen minutes passed. The nearest slip gap point along the slip tunnel they used is approximately thirty minutes away."

"What are you saying, Siggy?"

"That the math implies they were already en route when the Sarkonians landed on the planet."

"You think they signaled them when they were in orbit?"

"It is possible, but *The Star's* sensors didn't pick the Sarkonians up until a short while ago, moments before they arrived."

"Do you think the Union knew we were there before the Sarkonians even showed up?"

"It certainly appears that way, sir, but I cannot be certain. Not without additional data."

I glanced at the bobblehead of Foxxy Stardust on my dash. Her head was still bouncing from the launch. "Well, you keep trying to get that data. I'll check on the rest of the crew."

I unhooked my harness straps and pushed myself onto my feet. I could already hear people talking in the lounge, even before the door was open.

"—need to get Octavia to another hospital," Freddie finished saying.

"Not until we know we're safe," said Abigail.

"But what if she needs more treatment?" asked Hitchens, who was standing beside Octavia's chair.

Lex was there, too, watching the others talk. She glanced at me and smiled, then ran over to greet me. "Mr. Hughes!"

"Hey, kid," I said.

"Can we go somewhere fun? I'm tired of being on the ship."

"Wish we could," I answered, patting her on the head. "Hopefully it won't be long before we land again."

She frowned, clearly disappointed by the answer.

"Tell you what, though," I went on. "Gimme ten minutes and I'll grab you some jerky and cheese."

Her eyes lit up at the prospect of food. "Can I, um, can I have some tomato soup?"

"Sure, kid." I walked past her and toward the others, who were still discussing options in the middle of the lounge.

"I just don't—" Freddie stopped when he saw me. "Captain Hughes, is everything okay now? Did we take any damage?"

"You'd know it if we had," I said.

"What about that Union ship?" asked Abigail.

"What about it?" I asked.

"Is it pursuing us? Are we safe?"

"Beats me. We won't know until we're at the next S.G. Point."
I looked at Octavia. "How about you?"

"Me?" she asked.

"Are you holding up all right?"

"I can't feel my legs. What do you think?"

"I think if you can still be sarcastic, things can't be that bad."

"Fair point," she said.

"As for the plan, I figure we'll stick to the map," I continued.
"The atlas we got from that cave has us heading this way. We'll
just stay on course and keep our eye on the prize."

"You act like it's such a simple thing," said Abigail. "Like trying
to win something out of one of those stuffed toy machines."

"Since when are those things easy?" I asked.

"I don't know, but compared to running for our lives, I'd
imagine they can't be that bad."

"I have a cloaked ship, if you'll remember," I said.

"Do you think that will be enough?" she asked.

"Trust me. When we get out of this tunnel, we'll go dark and
bide our time. No one will know where we've gone, and if they
ever do figure it out, we'll have disappeared completely."

THREE

I sat in my room, my feet on my desk as I leaned back in my chair, playing with the gold pocketwatch Abigail had given me. It had a planet engraved on it, which she'd called Earth. I didn't know if I believed the myth, but I still liked the watch. She'd given this to me, believing she'd never see me again.

That was before we went on the run together. Now, we were crewmates, all of us, the road before us full of unknown possibilities.

The territory ahead was largely owned by the Sarkonians, but their borders were constantly in flux. For all I knew, we'd already crossed over. The bastards loved claiming systems that were nowhere near their own space.

But the universe was a big place, and they could only go in so many directions. If we stayed on this path, we'd cross through their space in a matter of days. If I kept *The Star* cloaked, we'd have an easier time of it.

A soft knock at my door stirred me, and I dropped my feet and stowed the pocketwatch. "What is it?" I asked.

"It's Fred. Do you have a minute?"

"No," I answered. "I'm busy watching a holo. Ever heard of *Lustful Sins of a Sarkonian Wife*?"

There was a short pause. "Oh, I, uh, I don't—"

I hit the door control and it slid open, revealing Freddie's stammering face. "What is it, Freddie?"

"A-Are you really watching that?"

"I will if you don't hurry up," I cautioned.

"I..." He paused, taking a breath. "I have a small request, if you don't mind."

"What is it? You need to have the talk? I suggest you try Hitchens. I'm not really the fatherly type."

"I want you to teach me how to shoot."

The words lingered in the air a moment, taking me by surprise. "What did you just say?"

He cleared his throat. "Look, Captain, I'm no fool. I know you ordered me to stay back because I'm useless in combat."

He wasn't wrong. The poor guy had practically no experience to speak of when it came to fighting. I wagered he wouldn't be able to hit a wall of *The Star* if I gave him a rifle and pointed. "I don't know if I have time for that kind of thing."

"Please, Captain," he begged. "I don't want to be on the sidelines while the rest of you pick up my slack."

Call me a sucker, but I felt for the kid. He wasn't raised like me. He didn't grow up on the street, getting in knife fights at the age of nine. "Before you joined that cult, did you ever have to use a gun, Freddie?"

"Once or twice," he said, hesitantly.

"Ever have to kill anyone?"

He shook his head.

"That could be a problem. I'm not sure I have the time to get rid of that part of you."

"What part?" he asked.

I poked him in the chest. "*That* part. You know, the thing inside that makes you afraid to murder some asshole before he can murder you."

"Murder? But it's self-defense, isn't it?"

"Sometimes it's business. Sometimes it's preemptive," I explained. "You do what you gotta do out here, Freddie. That's how it works."

His eyes widened. "Gods, Captain. Is that how you've been living this whole time?"

"It's the only way to live. It's how you stay alive. Make no mistake, Fred. This ain't the Union or your church. It's the fucking void. There ain't any rules out here. No civilization to tell you how to exist. You take what you take, kill who you kill, and try to make it out alive."

I wanted the weight of my words to sink in. I wanted him to understand. Killing wasn't easy, but a second of hesitation could make you a corpse.

But...it's necessary," he muttered. "It's how I protect the rest of you. Isn't that right?"

I nodded. "It's how a crew survives. We do it together. We look out for each other. But you gotta be willing to pull that trigger."

He stood there for a moment, and I could see the wheels turning in his head. He was convincing himself that this was right, justifying what he had to do. "Okay," he finally told me. "I understand, Captain."

"Good," I said. "Because if you get me killed, Freddie, I swear to the gods, I'll fucking rise from the grave and come back for you. Do you understand?"

* * *

I spent the afternoon showing Freddie how to aim a rifle. I had noticed his posture a few times, most recently back in the hospital, and thought it would be a good place to start.

Once I was satisfied that he wasn't going to accidentally recoil the weapon into his nose, I went about the business of explaining how to aim. "You want to keep your breath steady. It's cliché and everyone knows it, but hey, it's also true."

"What do you mean?" he asked.

I placed my hand on my chest. "Breathe out, but keep it steady," I said, exhaling. "The point is to keep yourself balanced. You need your calm."

"My calm?"

"Every seasoned soldier gets it after being in the shit for a while. It's a state of mind. That's the best way I can explain it."

"What is it?"

I'd never explained this sort of thing before, so it took me a second to find the right words. "When you're running, you know how your heart is racing?"

"Sure, adrenaline kicks in," he said, nodding.

"Right, exactly. The same thing happens when you're in the shit, only it's about a hundred times worse. Your whole body tenses up. The synapses in your brain are lighting up like crazy. Your tongue gets dry. You get that sick feeling in your gut, like you're about to throw up. It's the same thing that happens before you fuck for the first time. It makes you clumsy and stupid, and it gets you killed in a quick hurry."

"How do you control that?" he asked.

"Practice," I said, simply. "And breathing. Lots of it. Every chance you get, you breathe. Take deep breaths when you're alone in your bunk, stop in the hall when no one's around. Just keep doing it."

"That's all I have to do?"

I laughed. "Fuck no, kid. You're gonna need to fight someone. Maybe get your face torn up. I don't know. It's gonna take time to get your calm."

"I see," he said, looking down at the rifle in his hands.

I was being hard on him, telling him all this, but he had to hear it. I liked Freddie, for whatever reason, and I didn't want him to die anytime soon. If those Union and Sarkonian bastards kept coming after us, he'd need his wits about him. He'd need to be willing to kill. "Where's the nun today?" I asked, after a moment.

"Are you referring to Sister Abigail?"

"Ain't no other nuns on the ship, so who else?"

"I believe she's teaching Lex her math tables."

I tapped the com in my ear. "Siggy, patch me through to Abigail's room."

"Right away, sir," said the A.I.

A second later, I had her. "What is it, Jace?" she asked, an obvious annoyance in her voice. "I'm busy."

"Too busy to help your pal Fred?" I returned.

"What's wrong? Is he okay?"

"He's fine. I need you to come down to the cargo bay."

"I'm on my way," she answered.

I clicked off the com, then took Freddie's weapon. "Give me that," I said, walking over to the nearby locker and putting it away. "Abby's on her way to help you out."

"Help me out?" he asked.

"I can't do everything, and I really don't have the time. You're like a newborn pup, Fred, sorry to tell you. You need a momma."

The door slid open at the back of the bay as Abigail entered. She walked down the steps and joined us in the center of the bay, her arms behind her head. "What's all this about?" she asked, raising an eye.

"I need you to beat the living shit out of Freddie here," I told her, motioning with my thumb. "Think you can do that?"

* * *

Abigail's fist slammed into Freddie's jaw so hard I heard a crack. Spit flew from his mouth as his cheeks rippled from the blow, and he yelped, staggering back.

"I told you to block me!" the nun yelled.

He fell on his ass and covered his quickly bruising face. "I-I wasn't ready!"

"You can't always be ready in a fight," I said, shaking my head and trying to sound disappointed. "So embarrassing."

"Are you hurt?" asked Abigail. She let out her hand to help him up.

Freddie got to his feet and, after checking his jaw, nodded. "I'll be fine."

"Ready to go again?" I asked.

"Again?" repeated Abigail. "Did you see what just happened?"

"I'm ready," interjected Freddie.

We both looked at him. "That so?" I asked, cocking my brow at Abigail. "Hear that? He's ready."

"I heard him," she said, glaring at me. "But if he's not careful, he could get seriously injured, and we can't have that if the Union finds us again."

"I can handle it," insisted Freddie. He put up his fists like a boxer.

I tried not to laugh.

Abigail ignored him. "Can I speak with you for a moment, Captain?"

"Sure." I followed her to the bay door in the back, a few meters inside the hall where Freddie couldn't see us. "Well, this feels familiar."

"Familiar?"

I recalled being here once before with Abigail, having another conversation about a passenger, only it was Lex instead of Freddie that time. She'd told me her situation was complicated…that she was in a bit of trouble, and I believed her because that's how it went out here. It was hard to think how far we've come since then. "Nothing," I said, not wanting to get into it. "What do you wanna say? I assume it's about Freddie."

She crossed her arms. "You need to take it easy on him."

"Easy?" I asked. "He's the one who asked for help."

"He's only doing that because he thinks he has to. You need to tell him it's not his job to fight."

"What is his job, anyway? Hitchens and Octavia are archeologists. You're some kind of crazy nun with a trigger finger. Lex is a freak kid with magical powers. I own the ship. What exactly does Freddie do?"

"He's an expert on the Church and the early writings of Darius

Clare."

"You mean the old guy who started the Church?"

"That's right," she said. "He practically has Dr. Clare's entire library memorized."

I raised my hands. "Oh, well I'm sure that's handy in a fight."

She narrowed her eyes. "You know that's not fair. He has other values."

"Not fair?" I repeated. "We're not on some pilgrimage. There's a giant fucking ship that's hot on our asses, trying to track us down and kill us. Well, kill *most* of us. I'm sure they'll just take Lex and leave the rest of us for—"

"I get it," she interrupted.

"Do you? Because if we're going to survive this suicide mission across the universe, we're going to need everyone on this ship trained and ready to fight. Freddie needs to know how to kill in a heartbeat. Do you want him hesitating when it's your life on the line?"

"Ugh, fine," she groaned. "I swear to the gods, Jace." She turned away from me and headed back inside. "Frederick, get ready."

"A-Are you going to hit me again?" asked Freddie.

I stepped into the bay and leaned against the railing above the stairs, watching Abigail descend. "She's going to kick your ass until you're better, Fred."

"Oh, boy," he said, taking a deep breath.

Abigail got into her fighting pose. "Ignore him and try to keep up."

FOUR

I left Abigail and Freddie to train, or rather, I left Freddie to get his ass kicked by a nun, and then made my way to the lounge.

Hitchens was there, sitting with Lex on the sofa. He had a box in his hands—one of the ancient relics we'd brought with us from the asteroid belt. He gave it to the girl and she took it, smiling, and the device instantly lit up, illuminating her face.

"Got yourself another toy?" I asked, crossing my arms and leaning against the wall a few meters from the couch.

"Ah, Captain! I was hoping to speak with you about something, whenever you had a chance."

"Looks like you're busy now," I said, nodding at the glowing square in Lex's hands. "Got yourself another music box?"

I made my way over to the snack bar, eying the place where my coffee-maker had been, back before Fratley and his goons roughed my ship up and broke half my furniture. I missed that delicious brew like nobody's business.

"Not quite," said the doctor. "This one's a little less playful. More like a—"

The box suddenly snapped open, its lid popping up. The

sound startled Lex, but she laughed soon after.

"A lockbox," finished Hitchens. He chuckled. "Time to see what's inside."

Lex peered into the opening. "What's that?"

Hitchens reached inside the container and brought out a smaller object. It was flat, like a pad, but it had no screen. "Strange," muttered the archeologist. "I haven't seen anything like this before."

"Is it a toy?" asked the little girl.

"Might be," he said, nodding. He looked at her and grinned. "What say we find out?"

She smiled. "Okay!"

Hitchens took the storage box from her and the light inside immediately dimmed, going dark after a few short seconds. He handed her the other, much smaller object, and she took it, curiously.

We all watched, waiting for something to happen. "What's the deal?" I asked after a minute had passed.

Hitchens tapped his chin. "It could be malfunctioning. I might need to replace some parts, although I don't know if I have them on hand. Lex, dear, could you place the device back inside the—"

A sudden burst of light exploded from the girl's hands, hitting the farthest wall, near the cockpit door.

I hit the floor, reflexively. "Holy fuck!"

Lex screamed, releasing the object. She recoiled, falling back into the sofa and kicking her legs. Hitchens wrapped his arms around her, shielding her from whatever the hell was happening.

The light vanished a short moment after it appeared, but that didn't stop the girl or Hitchens from panicking. I scrambled to my feet and kicked the little machine away from her, knocking it beneath the coffee-maker table. "Fuck!" I yelled.

Hitchens released Lex. "O-Oh, my goodness! Are you all right?"

"My...my hand," she muttered, tears streaming down her cheeks as she stared at her fingers. They were red and bloodied.

"Oh, dear," said Hitchens, carefully taking her hands in his. "Captain! Captain, Lex needs medical attention!"

I tapped my ear. "Siggy, tell Octavia to get her ass to the lounge! Get Abigail, too. She'll want to be here."

"Yes, sir," responded Sigmond.

"Can you bend your fingers?" asked Hitchens. He looked absolutely worried, but I could tell he was trying to hide it. "Try to make a fist if you don't mind."

"O-Okay," she said, doing as he asked. She squeezed her fingers together, flinching slightly, but still going through with it.

It reminded me how tough this little girl actually was, for better or worse.

Octavia came rolling down the hall in a matter of seconds. "What's going on?"

She came to a stop right in front of the sofa.

"Lex fried her hands," I said. "It's Hitchens' fault. He gave her one of those stupid relic things."

She leaned in close to Lex and took her wrist to examine the wound. "It looks like a burn," she said. "Doctor, is the Captain right? Did you do this?"

Hitchens frowned. "Oh, I'm so sorry. Yes, it's true, Octavia. I wasn't thinking. I'm so sorry, Lex."

"It's okay, Mr. Hitchens," said Lex, wiping her eyes on her shoulder. "It doesn't hurt as much anymore."

"It doesn't?" asked Hitchens.

"No, not as bad," she said, but then flinched when Octavia touched her.

"It looks like your fingers are pretty sensitive. We need to get some gel on your skin," suggested Octavia. "Doctor, can you bring her to my room? I'll get the medical kit."

"Right away," said Hitchens, getting off the sofa. "Let's do as Octavia says, Lex."

I watched him lead the girl down the hall. When they were close to the room, Octavia swiveled in her chair to look at me. "Where is it?" she asked.

"Where's what?" I returned.

"The device you mentioned. I assume it's still here."

"Right there, under the table," I said, motioning with my head.

She stared at it, curiously, before looking back at me. "Get rid of it."

"You don't want to keep and study it?" The statement surprised me, given her history as an archeologist, like Hitchens.

"Not if it's dangerous enough to do that. Did you see her fingers?"

"They looked fucked up, yeah."

"She has second degree burns, Captain. Those are serious injuries."

"She didn't act like it hurt that bad," I said.

"I expect she'll feel it soon, once the shock has settled."

I glanced down at the device on the floor, at whatever the fuck had just blasted a beam of light in my lounge. "Guess I should find somewhere to dump this."

* * *

I didn't toss the box. Instead, I stuck it back inside the container it came in, and then I stuffed that inside a closet inside my room.

Back on Taurus, my old pal Ollie (rest his soul) had told me that these relics were worth their share in credits. Maybe if I held onto this garbage, I could find a trader somewhere who desperately wanted it.

Hell, I had to pay for fuel somehow, didn't I?

"Exiting slipspace in ten minutes, sir," announced Siggy.

"On my way," I said, closing the closet door and leaving my room.

By the look of the lounge, everyone was most likely with Lex, no doubt concerned over her well-being.

They probably thought I was heartless to ignore her, but I knew better. That kid was tougher than most. She wasn't some soft little girl. She was strong. She had what it took to be here.

I'd seen it on her face, back when Fratley had come...back when I'd killed him, right on this very ship. Lex had seen it all, but none of it had fazed her. The only way a person got through something like that, especially a kid, was if they'd witnessed something worse.

Much worse, I wagered.

Lex had to know what death was, long before she'd ever come aboard this ship. A girl like that, stuck in a galaxy like this...it made sense that she'd seen a killing or two, long before I came around.

I smirked, walking through the hall. *Whatever your story is, kid, I'm glad you made it this far.*

We arrived out of slipspace shortly after I strapped into my chair. The emerald lightning of the rift disappeared behind us as the tunnel closed. "Activate the cloak, Siggy."

"Understood, sir. Would you like me to move us to the next tunnel entrance?"

"That'd be fine," I said. "We got any movement in the system?"

"Affirmative, sir. It seems there's a construction project occurring on the moon surrounding the nearby gas giant."

That was a surprise. I had assumed we'd be alone when we

got there. "Why didn't you tell me about this before we came in?"

"Apologies, sir, but this project hasn't been entered into the galnet universal map yet."

"Maybe they don't want the Union to know about it," I suggested. "Or the Sarkonians, for that matter."

"That is a possibility, sir."

"Can you run a deep scan and tell me what's there?"

"Already done," said Sigmond, anticipating my needs like always. "There appears to be a modest selection of shops in the local bazaar, as well as a fully functional fuel station."

A list of vendors came up on the holo, ranging from beer to clothes to beef-on-a-stick.

"If I might make a suggestion, Captain," continued Sigmond. "Our fuel reserves could use replenishing."

I thought about the fridge and the lack of food. "We might need more than that, now that you mention it, Siggy."

I heard a short knock on the door. "Mr. Hughes? Are you in there?" The door cracked open and I turned to see Lex peeking in. She kept most of her body behind the wall, afraid to enter. "Um."

"What is it, kid? Shouldn't you be resting from that blast you took?"

"That was a while ago," she said, hugging the door, bouncing a little. "What are you doing in here?"

"Finding us a place to wait." I turned away from her, back toward the console.

I heard her step inside, taking a seat next to me. "What are we waiting for?"

"Not sure yet," I muttered.

"Oh."

I glanced down at her hand. It was bandaged, delicately wrapped, probably by Octavia. "Your hand doing okay?"

"Huh? Oh…" She pulled her hand away and placed it in her lap, covering her fingers with her other palm. "Yeah, it's better."

"Better?" I asked. "Don't be modest, kid."

Her eyes dropped to the dash, like she was embarrassed.

We sat there a while, saying nothing. I kept thinking she would get up and leave, but she never did. After a while, I cleared my throat, tired of the silence. "Hey," I said, finally. "When your hand gets better, I've got a computer game you can use. It's a racer. You like racers?"

"What's a racer?" she asked.

"It's a game where ten ships see who's the fastest."

"Is it hard?"

"Depends how good you are. For me, it's easy. But for you…" I cocked my brow and shook my head. "It might be too much. You gotta be tough to handle a racer, you know."

"I'm tough," she said, sitting up straight. "I can do it."

"Really? You don't sound tough. How do I know?"

"I am!" she insisted. "I can do it!"

I tapped my chin. "Hm…yeah, you know, maybe you are

tough."

"Yeah," she said, quickly. "I promise I am."

"Well, once your hand is better, we'll have to find out. You can show me."

"But my hand is okay now!" She raised the bandaged appendage, no longer shy about it. "See? It's better!"

"I'm sure it is," I said, trying to sound like I believed her. "But let's give it more time to heal. You don't want it to be sensitive."

She furrowed her brow. "But it's better! Just look, Mr. Hughes."

She started to unwrap the bandage from around her fingers.

"Hey, kid, hold on a second," I cautioned. "You shouldn't do that."

Fuck, what was I thinking?

She took the bandages off in a hurry, letting them fall on the floor, between our seats. "See? Look, Mr. Hughes."

Lex lifted her hand in the air between us, fluttering her fingers. I had expected to see them inflamed, possibly charred and bloodied from the blast. Instead, they had a soft pinkness to them, like the skin of a newborn. I took her hand, steadying it so I could see. "What the hell?" I muttered, leaning in, searching for the burns. "What happened? Why isn't there—there's not even a scar."

Lex smiled. "Does this mean I can play the racer now?"

"Hold on," I said. "Siggy, did you get the incident in the lounge recorded? Answer privately."

"Of course, sir," I heard his voice say in my ear. "Would you like me to replay the footage?"

I glanced at Lex, who was staring at me, still smiling. It would probably be a bad idea to pull the feed up in front of her. She might be tough, but I didn't know if she'd be able to sit and watch herself get hurt. Besides, Abigail would fucking kill me.

"No," I finally decided. "Just run a quick analysis and tell me how bad the injuries were."

I took Lex's hand and rewrapped the bandage. For some reason, it felt like the best thing to do.

A few short seconds later, Siggy chimed in with an answer. "Octavia Brie's initial analysis was partially correct, sir. Lex received second degree burns, but there were also first degree burns along the index finger."

I swiveled in my seat, taking Lex's hand again and looking over her fingers. None of them appeared damaged, far as I could tell. "How long does a burn like that take to heal, Siggy?"

"Given the medical resources available on this vessel, I would place the estimate at six days. However, there could be scarring and some pigment discoloration afterwards."

I let Lex's hand go. It dropped to her lap, and she stared up at me with big, curious blue eyes.

I turned away from her, lowering my voice so it was hardly above a whisper. "Siggy, if there's supposed to be scarring or something, if it's supposed to be as bad as you said, do you have an explanation for why none of that has happened yet?"

He answered, "None whatsoever, sir."

FIVE

I asked Abigail and Octavia to meet me in the cargo bay, not long after my talk with Lex.

Octavia was sitting in her wheelchair, palms on her wheels. We had to stay on the upper deck, above the stairs, because I didn't have a ramp.

"What are we doing in here?" asked Abigail, leaning her ass against the rail. "Does this have something to do with why we stopped in this system?"

"We'll get to that," I said, not wasting any time. "First, have either of you seen Lex's hand?"

They both looked at each other. "What do you mean?" asked Octavia. "Are you talking about the bandage?"

"No, I mean what's under the bandage."

"There's a wound, last I saw," she responded.

"What's this about?" asked Abigail. "Captain, what exactly happened?"

"It's not what happened. It's what *didn't* happen."

She tilted her head. "What?"

I threw my finger out, pointing at the hall. "The kid's wounds are all healed up. There's no burns on her."

"No burns?" asked Octavia.

"None," I confirmed.

She paused, and I could see her trying to remember. "No, no, I saw them," she finally said. "She had serious degree burns all down her fingers."

"Not anymore. Her skin looks fine now."

"I'm sure you just didn't know what you were looking at," suggested Abigail.

"You want me to call her in here?" I asked. "She's in the lounge playing a game I gave her, but we can get her in here and you can see for yourselves."

"Hold on, Captain," said Octavia. "You're suggesting that her wounds healed in a matter of hours. Is that right?"

"I'm not suggesting anything," I corrected. "I'm *telling* you what I saw."

Abigail motioned at me. "But that is what you're saying, in your own weird way."

"There's no way those burns could have healed like that. It's not possible," said Octavia.

"Well, they did," I said, shrugging.

Abigail looked down at Octavia. "Maybe you were wrong about the diagnosis?"

"I don't think so." She pushed her wheels and swiveled around. "Let's go talk to her."

I stepped out of the way to let her past. For someone stuck in a chair, she sure was quick, rolling through the corridor, wheels clicking as they turned.

We found Lex exactly where I'd left her, sitting on the sofa playing on a small pad, tilting it left and right as she played. I could see her having a time of it, crashing her ship into the invisible barriers of the racetrack as she moved from one part of the solar system to the next. She was in thirteenth place, failing miserably.

Poor kid had no skills.

"Lex, honey, can we speak with you for a moment?" asked Octavia.

The girl looked up from the screen. "Huh? But I'm racing."

"It'll only take a second," said Abigail. "You can finish the game afterwards."

Lex frowned and looked at me with an expression that said, *Please Mr. Hughes, save me.*

I shrugged at her, saying nothing.

Lex dropped her head, defeated, and placed the pad on the sofa.

"Can we see your hand?" asked Octavia.

Lex nodded, and Octavia leaned in and carefully took her palm.

Abigail and I watched as she examined the girl's hand, unwrapping the bandage. Octavia's eyes widen, like she didn't understand what she was seeing, but she quickly composed herself. "Thank you, Lex," she said, calmly, and didn't bother rewrapping the girl's hand.

"Can I play now?" asked Lex.

"Go ahead," said Octavia. "But can you go in your room?"

She nodded, and leapt off the sofa, headed down the hall. We waited until she was out of sight before looking at one another.

"You see what I'm talking about?" I asked the two women.

"I'm sure the burn just wasn't that bad," said Abigail.

"This doesn't make sense," muttered Octavia, staring at the bandages.

Abigail sat on the couch, looking at the wrap, then at Octavia. "Are you certain you didn't simply make a mistake about—"

"I didn't," said Octavia, looking up at her. "I'm telling you, that girl had burns on her hands. The kind that don't heal in a few hours."

Abigail started to respond, but I cut in. "I had Siggy look over the footage. He said there was no way those burns could heal that fast."

"Sigmond, is that true?" she asked.

"It is," said the A.I., his voice filling the room.

"I just don't see how it's possible, though," said Abigail.

"Have you ever seen her recover this quickly before?" asked Octavia.

"Not to my knowledge," said Abigail, but then she hesitated, almost drifting in thought, like she wasn't entirely sure.

I could tell she was having a hard time remembering, so I tried asking the question in a different way. "Have you ever seen her get injured?"

The nun looked at me. "You know I have."

"Oh? Do I?"

"When that Fratley person came on our ship. Those men, they roughed her up."

"No," I corrected. "They roughed *you* up, not Lex. I saw the whole thing. Maybe you didn't, since you were knocked the fuck out."

"Careful, Captain," she said, giving me a look that suggested if I didn't shut up, I'd regret it.

"In any case," interjected Octavia. "Was there another time where she was injured under your watch?"

The bluntness of the question surprised me. She might as well have asked if Abigail was a neglectful guardian.

"No, nothing serious," said Abigail.

"We may need more information."

"What are you suggesting?" I asked. "You want to cut her? See how fast it takes to heal?"

Octavia was quiet for a minute. "No, we can't do that," she eventually said.

"What's your suggestion, then?" I asked.

She paused a second, looking down at the bandage that was still in her lap. She picked it up, and the bloodstained ends of the cloth fell against her arm. "I might have an idea."

* * *

Octavia called for Hitchens to join us in the cargo bay, suggesting he bring an electron microscope, along with Lex. He got there in a hurry, clumsily making his way through the corridor with the bulky equipment in his hands.

"Where shall I set it down?" he asked, breathing heavily as he stepped into the cargo bay. Lex was right behind him, carrying her little rocket ship, flying it in the air and making whooshing sounds.

"Preferably where I can reach," said Octavia.

"Ah, on the table, then." He waddled over to the side of the room, near the locker. "Here we are."

"Lex, honey, can you come here a moment?" asked Abigail.

The girl did as she was asked, running over to Abby's side. The nun took her hand and smiled.

Octavia motioned for her to come closer. "Can I see your hand again, Lex?"

"Uh huh," said Lex, extending her arm.

The assistant archeologist and former Union medic took a small device and placed it gently on the girl's wrist. It resembled a gun, in a way, with a trigger and a grip. She placed the barrel to the kid's skin, and I heard a soft click.

Lex didn't seem to notice, if there was even any pain. She used her free hand to continue playing with the rocket, flying the toy around her head, and smiling.

Octavia eventually let her go. "All done," she said. "You can go play now."

Lex didn't say anything, but instead ran back down the stairs and into the larger part of the bay.

"What's your plan here?" I asked, once the girl was far enough away.

"We're going to perform an analysis on her skin cells to see what we can find," said Octavia.

"What results are you expecting?" I asked.

"I'm not sure yet," she admitted. "We may not find anything at all, but there's something going on. I think we can all agree on that."

I nodded.

"How long will this take?" asked Abigail.

"Half an hour at most," she said. "You're welcome to—"

My earpiece clicked. "Sir, if you don't mind," interjected Sigmond. "There's a slipspace tunnel opening nearby."

I held up my hand to quiet the group, then touched the side of my ear. "Did you say a tunnel, Siggy?"

"That is correct. I'm running a scan now to determine the arriving vessel's classification code."

"I've gotta go," I said. "Stay here and play with your blood. Or skin. Or whatever. I'll be on the bridge."

"Is something wrong, Captain?" asked Hitchens.

"Someone just came out of slipspace, same direction we did. It could be trouble, but I don't know yet."

"Someone?" echoed Abigail. "But we aren't close to any colonies."

I could tell where she was going with this, and I would've been lying if I said it wasn't already in my head. If anyone had come this way, so far from any known colonies, there was a good chance it had something to do with us. That might not be a guarantee, but I wasn't taking the risk. Not today.

I started jogging towards the front of the ship, ordering Sigmond to lock the door behind me once I was inside the cockpit. I didn't have time for any distractions, whether it was from the nun or the kid. I had work to do.

"Siggy, what do we have?" I asked, grasping the controls, prepared to fire the quad cannon, should the need arise.

"I detect no incoming vessels," Siggy responded.

"None? Then why's there a tunnel opening?"

"Uncertain."

"Well, you better get certain right fucking now."

"Understood, sir. Continuing scans."

The rift closed after another moment, sealing the green waves away so that only the stars remained. I sat there, not even blinking. Just waiting like a jackass.

"Siggy?" I said. "Anything?"

"No sign of movement," he answered. "This is most unusual,

sir."

"Unusual?" I repeated. "When was the last time you saw a slipspace tunnel close without anyone coming through it?"

"I have no records of such an event."

"Neither do I," I muttered, staring through the display. I touched the console, wondering if maybe Sigmond's detection protocols were acting up. It had been a while since I had him updated. Maybe he'd missed something.

No, the secondary scans checked out, or at least matched the results Siggy had given.

Whatever was going on, it didn't sit right with me…and I knew better than to ignore that feeling.

SIX

Seven hours and two slip tunnels later, our scans detected a small moon colony near a system called Proxi Beta, called so because it was the lesser neighbor to Proxi Alpha.

The system was technically inside Sarkonian space, although there were only a handful of military ships in the area. That was because this colony was still under construction, which is why I'd chosen to come here. It would still be a few months before the system was bustling with enough activity to give me anything to worry about. Until then, I could refuel and resupply, then be on my way, all without anyone noticing.

Besides, the Sarkonians allowed traders to visit their outermost colonies, which they often set up as commercial zones. It helped keep their crumbling economy alive. Thanks to my Renegade contacts, and using the galnet, I was able to procure some credentials as a salvage operator. It was low key enough to avoid drawing attention, while also giving me a valid reason to be here, off in the middle of nowhere.

"Does everyone have their assignments?" asked Abigail, standing beside me in the cargo bay. *The Renegade Star* had just made landfall on the moon, entering its habitation dome and parking in the third-largest of its docking platforms. Spot 226.

Freddie nodded. "I'm on fuel."

"And we're to stay put," said Hitchens, referring to himself and Octavia.

"Right," confirmed Abigail. "Let's not take more time than we need. No sightseeing."

"I doubt there's much to see, anyway," I said.

"What are you two doing?" asked Freddie, motioning at the nun and me.

"We're on ship supplies," I answered.

"You mean food," said Octavia, giving me a look.

I raised my brow. "That might be part of it."

"You just want to eat and get drunk."

"I'm the captain of this rig and I get to decide what kind of rations we carry. End of story."

"Fine, but at least get something we can all enjoy. Not just meat sticks and all that overly processed garbage you're so fond of."

"I make no promises," I said.

Abigail clasped her hands together. "Okay, we'll reconvene at the ship in two hours. Let's move quickly." She glanced at me. "And try not to draw too much attention."

"Are you talking about me, nun?" I asked.

"Who else would she mean?" asked Octavia.

We left Lex on the ship with Octavia and Hitchens, much to her frustration. She didn't argue, though, when I told her.

It seemed the kid was catching on.

Freddie was just outside, filling the engine with fuel. He'd be the first to return, which meant all Abigail and I had to do was grab our supplies and hurry back. Not a big deal, barring any unforeseen circumstances, but I didn't anticipate anything crazy. We were in the middle of nowhere on a tiny little moon, no sign or hint of the Union. No cause for alarm.

In the meantime, I could load up on snacks and beer, maybe even find some candy.

Abigail and I entered through the large hangar opening of the colony, which was very clearly still under construction. There were metallic beams lying next to the walls, half-completed plaster, and essentially no cosmetic fixtures in place yet.

None of that had stopped thousands from coming here and filling its streets, of course.

The colony was made up of three domes. A central, larger dome, with smaller ones on each side. This was a common design choice for colonies this size, and I recognized it immediately. These things were sturdy enough to withstand their share of meteors, because they had to be, but not tough enough that they could handle a full-on assault. That kind of fortified structure would have taken years to build, unlike this, which had sprung up overnight, likely within the last two months. It wouldn't really take that much to destroy it, should the Sarkonians or the Union get the urge, but I got the impression that this place had been left off the galnet map for a reason.

"Welcome to Spiketown," yelled a man with a funny hat as we walked into the massive opening. "Would you care to buy a rifle today? You can't use them in town, but they're great for hunting on Decca Three, just a few systems from here. I see you have a handgun there. Might you want some extra ammunition? I've got plenty of—"

"Not interested," I said with a cold voice that suggested if he asked me again, I might pull out his esophagus.

"U-Understood, mister," he answered, slowly backing away.

A mess of scattered buildings had been built all throughout the dome, lined up side-to-side. "Wonder where the market is," I said, still scanning the streets.

Abigail walked up to the same man from before. "Hey, where are all the shops?"

"Oh, uh, down this street and to the left, but it's a walk. That's why I set mine up here, near the entrance. Pretty smart, right? That way I get to greet all you nice—"

She turned and walked away, leaving him alone to slowly trail off. "Down and to the left," she said, coming back to us.

"Simple enough," I remarked.

Octavia's voice popped into my ear over the comm. "Captain, we're going to ask around the hangar and see if we can find some medical supplies. I believe there has to be some sort of medical facility. I'll let you know what I find." There was a short pause. "Although I have my reservations on the quality."

"Use the com if things get too hairy," I said.

"Don't worry about us," said Octavia. "I can handle whatever happens. Focus on obtaining the other supplies."

I smirked. "You gonna beat them with your wheels?"

"Keep talking and I'll show you firsthand," she returned.

I laughed as I started walking, almost believing her.

Abigail quickened her pace to match mine as we strolled through the streets towards the market. It was a cold city, if you could even call it one, and it smelled of grease and burning rubber, a common side effect of this sort of construction. The streets teamed with residents and visitors, here for gods-knew-what, most of them in their job uniforms.

We curved around the street, making a left just as the gun merchant had suggested. The market came into view soon, its dozens of tents and hastily built shacks primed for our perusing. I caught a whiff of cooked meat after a moment, and it lingered in the air a while before disappearing. It smelled like charred, smokey beef. As we drew nearer, I spotted a flame-pit with skewers of meat resting on the open fire, and my mouth watered with anticipation.

Without a word to Abigail, I walked briskly to the merchant, waving a finger to get his attention. He nodded at me and removed one of the skewers.

I took the rod and tore into the largest piece of meat. It was rough and chewy, with a strange taste that I didn't recognize. It wasn't beef, like I had thought, or any kind of fowl that I knew, but something else. Nothing bad, though, not at all. In fact, you could've given me just about any sort of meat and I'd be satisfied.

"How is it?" asked Abigail.

I grinned with the flesh between my teeth. "Better than you'd expect," I said, biting off another chunk.

"Twelve credits," said the cook, holding up a pad.

I tapped my ear. "Siggy, transfer the money."

"Processing," said Sigmond. "Transaction complete."

The merchant looked at the pad, nodded, and smiled. "Good doing business with you."

"Can I just ask," I said, swallowing and taking another bite. "What is this?"

"Rombdin," he said, flatly.

I had never heard of that before, so I pressed him further. "What's Rombdin?"

"You never heard of it?" he asked.

"Should I? Is it a type of bird or something?"

"Vermin," he said with a shrug. "Like a rat."

Abigail was standing behind me and gasped, suddenly. "A what?!"

"Vermin," the man repeated. "What? You don't like?"

I stared down at the meat that was still left on my stick.

"Jace, put that down!" said Abigail, utter disgust in her voice. "We can't eat any of this food. How horrible!"

My stomach growled as my eyes lingered on the skewer. "But..."

She shook her head. "This is what happens when you don't ask more questions before you dive into a situation."

"But..."

"What? Don't tell me you're thinking about eating the rest of that. Do you know what kind of diseases it might be carrying?"

"No diseases," said the merchant. "If you cook rombdin, it kills everything."

My mouth salivated at the sight of the meat, its charred skin blending with salt and spice.

"Jace, please, you're going to get sick if you—"

I tore into the remaining meat, ripping the tough Rombdin flesh and scarfing it. I barely chewed before swallowing.

I raised the skewer and grinned. "Another!"

The merchant returned my smile and handed me a second helping.

Abigail's mouth dropped and she looked away. "I can't watch this!"

When I had my fill of the rat-like food, I set the rods on the stone next to the fire pit and got to my feet. "Ready to go? I need to walk this off." I smacked my belly.

She wouldn't even look at me. "You smell like vomit. You know that, right?"

I grinned. "Smells like a win to me."

* * *

Abigail insisted we only buy food that was shipped and imported, sealed and frozen. I tried to argue in favor of bringing some fresh Rombdin back with us, but she wasn't having it, so I let it go.

After loading a cart's worth of supplies, I decided I wanted to take a piss, so I told Abigail to stay put while I took care of business.

The nearest restroom was a walk, but there was an alley between two buildings and I didn't want to wait. I also didn't see the harm, since it smelled like piss anyway. Leaving the street, I entered the narrow passage and got straight to it.

Right as I was finishing and zipping up my pants, I heard something move behind me. I turned, my hand on my pistol, ready to draw.

It was a young woman, dressed in rags, holding an object beneath her arm. "Oops," she said, nearly bumping straight into me.

I slid out of the way. "Who are you supposed to be?"

"D-Don't mind me, mister," she said, quickly. "Sorry if I scared you."

"You didn't." I looked at the box under her arm. It had a unique design on it, with layers of metal overlaying one another, similar to the ancient artifacts Hitchens had found. "Whatcha got there?"

"Oh, um, it's nothing," she said.

The box, if that's what it was, seemed about the size of my head, give or take. A little bigger than the one Lex had been playing with when she burned her hands. "What are you doing with it?" I asked.

"My father has a shop. You can buy it if you want. We have more of them."

"How much?"

"I don't know. You have to ask him. He's in charge."

I toyed with the idea of stealing it right there, but pushed the impulse away. Abigail would kill me if I swiped something from a kid. "Can you take me to your shop?"

"Uh, sure, mister. You really wanna buy it?"

"I don't know yet, but maybe."

She continued toward the street, motioning for me to follow.

Abigail was still standing next to the little cart with the rest of our supplies. I used the com to tell her what I was doing, since the crowd would only slow me down and I wanted to keep pace with the girl.

"What do you mean, you're going to see about a box?" she asked.

"It's some sort of relic. Looks a lot like the one Hitchens and Lex were messing with. I figure they might be useful to get. Just take the supplies back and I'll meet you at the ship."

She scoffed. "If you think I'm letting you run off like that, you're crazy," she said. "I'll be right there. Sigmond, please send me Jace's location."

"Understood," said Sigmond.

I almost cursed, annoyed at having a potential babysitter, but let it go. "Where's this place at, kid?" I asked the girl in front of me as we crossed the street.

She pointed to a medium-sized tent, just ahead of us—red and purple, with event posters stuck to its sides. Apparently, there was a cage match between Mayfew and Cole tomorrow night, two raves a few hours later, and Doro's Grill was having a sale for the next week. Based solely on the advertisements, I was starting to think this was my kind of town.

"I'm back," said the girl, rushing into the tent.

I followed, entering through the open flap.

"Welcome back, Camilla," said a bulking man behind the counter. He had a thick beard that filled out so well you might think he never shaved a day in his life, like he'd been born with it. His forearms were thicker than calves, with a chest so large I wondered why he was working here instead of fighting in a gladiator match on some other world. For all I knew, maybe he once had.

"This man wants to ask you about the stuff from the pit," said Camilla.

"Is that so?" asked the burly fellow. He extended his hand to me. "Bolin Abernathy. Good to meet you, stranger."

I shook his hand. "Jace," I said, simply.

"What can I do for you, Jace? Are you really interested in buying those boxes?"

"Might be," I said. "Depends on the price."

He raised his eye. "What can you offer?"

"Not much, I'm afraid. I'm just a scrapper, so I don't have too many credits, but I'll pay what I can if the price is fair."

He nodded like he understood. "How about we start with this one and go from there?" He tapped his palm on the box his daughter had brought in.

"Sure," I said. "How's fifty creds?"

"That's not a bad starting offer. Could you do one hundred?"

I twisted my lip. "Eh, I don't think so. I can't get much out of them at that rate. Really, anything over sixty is tough."

"Sixty, huh?" asked Bolin. "Well, maybe we can do that price, but you'd have to get more than one."

"How many do you have?"

"This is the only box like this, but we got plenty of other makes," he said, patting his daughter on the head. "My little Camilla salvages them from the dig sites, but there's not much to speak of. I only have seven others."

"So, that's eight total?" I asked.

"Right, but like I said, only one is a box."

I nodded, pretending to really think this over. "That's a tough call. Sixty credits each will set me back." I had, of course, already decided to buy them. I could probably resell these for ten times that on the free market. "You know what, sure. I'll do sixty each, but I need to see the rest of them first."

Bolin smiled. "A wise decision, my friend!"

"I hope so," I said.

"Camilla, go and get some of the others," said Bolin.

She smiled and ran off, into the second part of the tent, behind him.

"If you don't mind me asking, how'd a guy like you end up scrapping in a place like this?" I asked.

He chuckled. "I'm not just a scrapper. I also work for the trading company here. I'm in construction." He laughed again. "Actually, almost all of us are."

"What else are they building here?" I asked. "Don't tell me it's just a triple dome, because this is really out of the way for a little colony."

He nodded. "The way I heard it, there used to be something else here, maybe a thousand years ago. I'm not sure, but the company I work for decided it wanted to dig. So far, they haven't found much of anything, but they keep going anyway."

A thousand years ago? I thought. *That certainly explains the artifacts.*

Right at that moment, I heard footsteps behind me at the tent entrance. I looked to see Abigail poking her head inside, probably checking to make sure I was here. "There you are," she said.

"Is this your wife?" asked Bolin.

Both Abigail and I looked at one another. "Oh, uh, she's—"

"Yes, we're married," she said, interrupting me.

I narrowed my eyes at her with a disjointed expression. "Huh?"

"We're on our way to my uncle's place, but Jace here insisted on stopping for fuel. Next thing I knew, he wanted to see what shops were here." She shook her head. "I see he's found another one."

Bolin laughed. "I was just talking to your husband about scrapping. It seems we share the same interest."

"Is that right?" she asked, looking at me. "Isn't that a strange coincidence."

"It is," I said, simply.

"And what exactly did you manage to *scrap* this time?"

"He wanted to purchase a few of these," said Bolin, pointing to the box.

Abigail's eyes widened at the sight of the artifact. She recomposed herself quickly, but I knew there was more to this, whatever the hell it was, and it made me even more curious. "Oh, well, as long as he can wrap this up soon, I'd like to be on our way.

My uncle is probably worried."

"I'll have you ready to go as soon as possible," Bolin assured her.

I heard a click on my com. "Captain, it's Doctor Hitchens. Are you available or otherwise engaged?"

I touched my ear. "What is it, Doc?"

"Octavia and I have had no luck procuring any proper medical research supplies. It seems this city is still under construction and does not have a working hospital or even an emergency medical station. Of all the facilities to delay construction on, one would think—"

"Was there something else or was that all you needed?" I asked, cutting him off.

"Oh, pardon me. Octavia managed to discover the whereabouts of a medical research space station, not far from here. It also happens to be along our present heading."

"And you think that will help us with Lex?"

"If the station has the right supplies and equipment, I believe so, Captain."

I looked at Abby. "Thoughts?"

"I think it's a good move," she said.

"Okay, you got that, Siggy?" I asked. "Update our route when you have a chance."

"Understood, sir. I shall do so immediately."

Finally, things were looking up. We had promises of artifacts and a proper lab to test the kid, maybe find some answers. I wondered if it was safe to start feeling optimistic, but buried the feeling.

Optimism made a person feel safe. It was the fastest way to get yourself killed. I couldn't have that.

"Is everything okay?" asked Bolin.

I'd forgotten he was there. Oops. "Yeah, nothing to be concerned about. I was just talking to a friend. He's on our ship and was hoping to restock our medicine. No luck here, though."

"Oh, I see. Is he a doctor? I heard you call him 'Doc'."

"Something like that," I said, but left it at that.

Camilla came back, carrying several smaller pieces in her arms. I didn't recognize any of them, but it definitely seemed like the same sort of technology we were after. Part of me wanted to call Hitchens and Octavia to have them give their opinion, but doing so might make Bolin suspicious and I couldn't have him raising the price or calling someone. The last thing I needed was a background check and my warrant popping up on a screen with hundreds of thousands of credits enticing these people to turn me in.

"Thank you, Camilla," said Bolin, helping her set the objects on the nearby table. "Please, folks, have a look."

I eyed each of the relics, pretending like I knew what I was doing. I caught Abigail doing the same, although she was trying to seem uninterested. It would have been better if we'd gone into this prepared, our roles reversed, with her acting as the scrap expert and me as the clueless husband, but I couldn't go back now. Besides, I didn't live with regrets. "Some of these are decent, but I don't know about the rest," I muttered, sweeping my fingers across my jaw, like I was in deep thought. "Tell you what, how about I buy the lot from you in bulk at, say, three seventy-five?"

"Three hundred and seventy-five credits?" he asked.

I nodded. "That's a fair price for what you have."

He glanced at each of the devices, probably trying to gauge the value, but I knew he had no idea. No one in this tent knew what this shit was worth. Not really. "I can do that," he said, after a few seconds. "Yes, I can do that."

"Great, then it's a deal. All your pieces for three hundred and seventy-five credits."

"I'll get the account pad and you can make the transfer," he said, reaching beneath the counter. "Was there anything else you wanted to—"

A loud pop went off somewhere in the distance, sounding like a gunshot.

I turned where I stood, hand at my waist. "The hell was that?!"

"Uh, oh!" said Camilla, hiding behind her father. "Is it the Rakers?"

"The *what*?" I asked.

"Rakers," repeated Bolin. "The Sarkonian military stationed here. They come around sometimes, looking for illegal trading."

"Illegal trading?" I shot another look at the relics. "Are you allowed to have these?"

Bolin scratched the back of his head. "Um."

I slammed my open hand on the table. "Quick, get this shit wrapped and stowed before they get here!"

He didn't argue, probably because he knew the Sarkonian military didn't fuck around. He took everything in a large brown sack and ran to the back, along with his daughter. I heard lids opening and shutting as they frantically tried to hide the evidence.

Just then, the tent flap flew open. Abigail and I turned to see three soldiers storm in, each holding rifles across their chests. They were dressed in Sarkonian armor, the same uniforms we'd seen at the hospital. "Everyone stop where you are!" barked one of them, a woman with a thin scar across her cheek.

Abigail and I turned toward them and raised our hands, slowly stepping to the side and away from the counter. "Just shopping here," I told her. "No need to blow our heads off."

"Where's the shop owner? Get out here right now!" barked the female officer.

Bolin came quickly from the back half of the tent, opening the halfway flap, sweat on his forehead. "S-Sorry about that," he managed to say. "I was trying to find some engine parts for this man here."

"Engine parts?" asked the officer, glancing at me. "You have a ship?"

"I do," I said.

She eyed me. "You don't look like a resident. What's your business?"

"My wife and I are on our honeymoon, headed to see her uncle. We thought we'd stop here on the way to see what goods you had to trade. I figured I could use some replacement parts while I was here."

"I see," said the officer, staring at us for what felt like a creepily long time. For a moment, I could have sworn I saw one of her eyes flicker, but convinced myself it was only my nerves. "Well, mind your business in this town and you'll be fine, but I need you to stay where you are for now. We're performing a search on all the shops here."

"Is that what the gunshot was about just now?" I asked.

"Someone gave us trouble. Better not to do what they did."

"Right, of course." I looked at Abigail. "We won't be a problem. Right, dear?"

"Goodness, no," said Abigail, her voice suddenly much softer than I was used to hearing. "Oh, dear me, you know, I just don't want to cause anyone any trouble."

I blinked at her, surprised by whatever the fuck she was doing. She sounded like a completely different person.

"Mr. Abernathy, is it? Our records show you have a daughter. Where is she?" asked the officer.

"Sleeping. She's been there for hours," he said.

"Bring her out here right now."

"I-Is that necessary, ma'am?" he asked.

"It is if you don't want to get arrested. Now, do as I say."

He looked at us, concern all over his face, and slowly backed away into the rear section of the tent. A moment later, he returned with his daughter, who was rubbing her eyes like she'd just woken up.

I had to give her credit. The girl could act. Even her hair was messy.

The female officer approached the two of them. With her rifle in hand, she looked down at the young girl. "Camilla Abernathy?"

"Yes," she answered, staring up at the woman.

"Please step out from behind the counter."

Camilla slowly came around the side of the table, looking both confused and terrified. We all knew where this was going.

The officer motioned at her two accomplices. "Take her."

The men grabbed the girl's wrists and place them behind her back.

"What's going on?" I asked.

"This child is under arrest for trespassing. We caught her on a holo recording, just behind the security fence."

Bolin's expression change to horror. "No, that wasn't her! She's been here all day!"

"Don't try to lie to me. I saw the feed myself. There's no mistaking it was her. In fact, I suggest you bring me the object she stole, unless you want us to shoot both of you where you stand."

"W-Wait!" pleaded Bolin. "I'm telling you, I didn't see her bring anything back. Don't hurt her!"

The woman nodded to her subordinate. "Have a look back there. See what you can find."

He did as she said and went into the rear of the tent. I heard some heavy shuffling as he tore the place apart, breaking what sounded like pottery. A few moments later, he returned with a wrapped cloth, full of the trinkets Bolin had shown us, all in one hand. In the other, he held the box.

"As I thought," said the female soldier.

Camilla started breathing quickly as the panic set in. Her eyes darted to the officer and then to the exit, and her foot began to edge forward.

I could already see what she was thinking. The problem with that, of course, was that she wouldn't get far if she ran. Amateurs never did. She'd run out of here, make it about twelve meters, and then a bullet would stop her dead in her tracks.

I sighed, removing my pistol from under my coat and aiming the barrel at the woman's face, cocking it. "That's good and plenty, I think," I said. "Let the girl go."

Abigail looked at me with total surprise. She obviously hadn't expected me to intervene, but it only took a moment for her to adjust. She drew her own weapon, holding it toward one of the other soldiers.

"What do you think you're doing?" asked the female officer. "Are you trying to get yourself killed?"

"You might not be that far off. Now, let the kid go."

She didn't seem fazed by the fact we had two weapons aimed at her team. "Do you know who you're talking to right now?"

"A Sarkonian," I said.

"I'm Commander Mercer Equestri. You will do as I say, unless you want to—"

I jerked my arm to the left and fired a quick shot into one of the other soldiers' legs. He fell to his knees with a loud scream.

Mercer Equestri looked at me with a wide-eyed expression. "What did you do that for?!"

"He was going for his weapon. Not a smart move."

The man screamed again, clutching his leg in pain. I raised my pistol back to the so-called commander.

"If you think I'm just going to hand this girl over to you, you're out of your mind!" she said.

I shrugged. "Sounds to me like you want a bullet in your chest."

She clenched her teeth, looking at Camilla, who was standing next to her in the other soldier's arms.

"Last chance, lady," I said.

She hesitated, then shook her head. "Let her go."

The other soldier released the girl.

"Give her that box, too, while you're at it," I said.

"That is the property of the Sarkonian government!" insisted Mercer.

"Do it or I'll shoot both of you in a different limb."

She gave me a look that either meant she wanted to kill me or bed me. Either way, I wasn't interested. "Give it to her," Mercer finally said.

The soldier handed the box to Camilla, and I motioned for her to come to my side. When she was close enough, I leaned down and whispered, "Get to the hangar. Spot 226. You understand?"

She nodded. "Okay."

I held her shoulder so she didn't go running off. "Wait a second," I whispered, then aimed my gun at the tent's flap, and fired.

The shot tore through the fabric, hitting something on the other side. A body fell on the ground, right in front of the entrance. He let out a groan.

"Always look for the rear guard," I told the girl. "Standard search and seizure. Now, you can go, kid."

She ran forward, jumping over the fallen soldier and taking off down the street.

Mercer watched the girl leave. "We'll find her soon. There are over two hundred active security personnel in this city and each of them has access to the same alert system I do. They'll know who she is the second our sensors pick up her biometrics."

I stepped closer to her, keeping the pistol on her at all times, and removed her rifle, throwing the strap over my shoulder. I also took the gun from the guy with the bullet in his leg. Once both weapons were safely removed, I turned Mercer around and put my barrel to the small of her back. "Whatever you say," I told her.

Abigail did the same with the other, yet-to-be-shot soldier, wrapping his arms behind him and taking his gun.

"Hey, Bolin, buddy," I began. "Got any cuffs we can use? Anything like that?"

"I, uh, I have some plastic ties," he said, crouching behind the counter.

As he brought them over to me, I felt Mercer tense up. "Must be tough, not being in control," I said, taking one of the straps from the shopkeeper.

"You're the one not in control," she said.

"Sure, lady, sure." I took her left wrist and wrapped the strap around it, making certain it was nice and tight.

She leaned back to look at me, a slight smile on her face. "You must be from the Union or somewhere in the Deadlands, is that right?"

"Shut up," I ordered. "It doesn't matter where I'm from."

"You're not that familiar with Sarkonian uniforms, are you?"

I snapped the second half of the tie around her other wrist, finally securing her hands. "I swear, lady, you must just want a bullet, the way you keep talking."

"Do yourself a favor, whoever you are, and look beneath the

small flap beneath my jacket. The one with the button."

I glanced at her stomach, following her eyes. "Why?"

"Just look," she said. "It's important for you to know."

"If this is a trap, I'm going to shoot you. You know that, right?"

She nodded. "Of course, and I promise, it's not."

I slid my finger to the button and unhooked it, lifting the flap of clothing, revealing a small piece of metal no larger than my thumb. "What is this?"

"A voice recorder. My personal identifier. A number of things, really, packaged into one."

"This thing is recording us?" I asked, jerking my hand back.

"And it just scanned your face," she said, with a wry smile. "Oh, look at that."

I saw a small reflection in her iris change. It must've been an implant for constant data retrieval. I'd heard of those before. Kept meaning to pick one up for myself, actually, but they were tough as shit to find on the market these days.

"Jace Hughes of *The Renegade Star*, is it?" she asked. "Looks like there's a hefty price on your head. Maybe I won't have you killed after all. Maybe I'll only rough you up before I arrest you." She glanced at Abby, and I saw another flicker in her eye. "Abigail Pryar, too. Wow, it looks like the bounty for you is even higher."

I ripped the recording device from her clothes and dropped it on the floor, stomping and cracking it.

"It's too late for that, Captain Hughes," said Mercer. "The rest of my security personnel are already being dispatched."

Abigail grabbed my arm. "We need to go!"

I pressed the barrel of my gun to the officer's temple. It had to hurt, but she smiled through it. "Call them off!" I told her.

"Not a chance, Hughes."

I started to squeeze the trigger, slightly pressing my finger to it, but stopped. A dead Sarkonian commander would only incentivize their fleet to hunt me down.

She smiled. "Smart move, Captain. You don't want to add homicide to your record. That would be—"

I smashed the butt of my gun into the side of her face, sending her to the floor. She might not eat a bullet today, but that didn't mean I couldn't give her a headache. She collapsed in front of me, seemingly unconscious.

Abigail gasped. "Holy!"

"Tie these idiots up and let's go!" I looked at Bolin. "Help me with the other guy."

"Okay, right," said the shopkeeper. The two of us dragged the bleeding soldier to the counter, wrapping his arms around one of the table legs and securing him. "What do we do now?" he asked.

"We get our asses out of here, that's what," I said, checking outside the tent. "And you're coming with us."

Seven

A bullet pierced the tent as soon as I opened the flap. I counted six soldiers, although I couldn't be certain, given the panicking crowd. "We have a problem!" I said, lifting my gun. "Abby, grab Bolin and let's go!"

"On it!" she returned, taking the shopkeeper by the arm. He was twice her size, but it was clear from the look on both their faces who exactly was in control.

"What are we doing?!" he asked.

"Running," said Abigail, tugging him along. "Stay close and try not to get shot!"

The enemy soldier's next blast struck Abigail's cart, a meter to my left.

I returned fire, getting his chest, knocking him on his ass, but the other five were still coming.

"Move!" I yelled, running.

Abigail and Bolin followed, and the three of us bolted through the street in the direction we'd arrived. We had to get to the ship as fast as possible or risk the rest of this godforsaken army coming down on us.

More gunfire from behind as we neared the end of the first street, but I didn't stop, not even to return fire. Not yet. There was no time, not when the entire city was about to go on high alert. We had to—

"Jace!" yelled Abigail, stopping a few meters after the turn. "Stop!"

"What the hell for?!" I asked, turning to see her holding Bolin, his arm around her shoulder. He was holding his other hand up, blood dripping from the place his finger used to be.

"Problem!"

I doubled back, almost sliding in the gravel. It took me a few seconds to get to them. "Can you keep going?"

"I-I think...I think so," Bolin said.

I grabbed the rag from his pocket and wrapped it around his fucked-up hand. "Keep your shit together and move!"

The soldiers weren't far behind us. There wasn't enough time to deal with a gunshot.

As if to answer me, Abigail said, "We can't leave him here, Jace!"

"Dammit, Abby," I said, taking the shopkeeper's other arm and throwing it over my shoulder.

We kept moving, trying to keep our pace. A siren began ringing through the intercom system in the dome. "EMERGENCY ALERT. CRIMINAL ACTIVITY IN PROGRESS. PLEASE RETURN TO YOUR HOMES."

"That must be us," I said as we stumbled through the street. I tapped the com in my ear. "Siggy, can you hear me?"

"Yes, sir," answered Sigmond.

"Start the goddamn ship! We're almost there!"

"Of course, sir. Preparing for launch."

"What about the others?" asked Abigail.

"Siggy, where's the rest of the crew?" I asked.

"With the exception of yourselves, all personnel are safely aboard the ship, sir."

"Good, tell everyone to strap in and get ready. We're almost there."

"Acknowledged, sir."

I glanced behind me and spotted a few soldiers making the turn to our street. "Hurry up!" I barked.

The exit was just before us. A dozen more meters and we'd be in the clear.

Shots fired from behind. "Stop where you are!" yelled one of the men.

I let go of Bolin's arm. "Get him on the ship!" I said. I pulled out my pistol and fired a quick two shots. "I'll be there in a second!"

Abigail didn't bother arguing. Maybe she finally understood how orders worked. "Fat chance," I said, popping another two shots off.

I dropped behind a nearby vehicle, hoping it would make decent cover, and continued firing at the soldiers. The first shot went wide and shattered a storefront window, but the second and third hit one in the shoulder and thigh. The fourth hit struck a soldier's rifle and nearly knocked him on his ass.

I took cover again, reloading.

A steady stream of bullets continued to fly above my head, bursting out the glass and rocking the vehicle. I felt the impact through my body as I kept my head down and hugged the front of the car.

I leaned beneath the vehicle's underbelly, firing six shots in quick succession and hitting two of the men in the feet. The second they hit the ground, I unloaded on them. "Siggy, if you have any ideas on how to get out of this, I'm all ears!"

"One moment, sir. I'll attempt to hack their security network to cancel the alert."

"That won't do any good! What about the people trying to kill me?"

"I'm afraid there's nothing I can do about that, sir."

I reached inside my belt and withdrew my emergency smoke grenade. "Fuck me," I muttered, throwing it over the back of my head.

It landed a few meters in front of the still-standing soldiers. "Grenade!" yelled one as they scrambled to take cover.

Using the hood of the car, I leveled my barrel and fired rapidly into the smoke. I couldn't see anything, but several screams followed.

A good sign.

I heard a voice from close by. "What are you doing?!"

I snapped my eyes around.

Not far from my position, sitting behind one the stalls, I saw the same merchant who'd tried to sell me weapons when I first entered this godforsaken town. He was hiding beneath his stall, looking at me with a rattled expression. "Get your ass out of here before you get yourself killed, moron!" I told him.

"I can't leave my merchandise!" he said. "What did you do to piss off security?!"

"I shot one of them," I said, pulling my pistol around my head and firing three more shots. I heard a scream and guessed I landed one.

Bullets continued to strike the side of the vehicle, denting the metal and popping two of the tires.

I reached for another magazine, but noticed I was out.

The merchant ducked behind his stall when a Sarkonian bullet nearly blew his head off. A second later, he leaned out the other side.

"Got any ammo back there?" I asked him, quickly.

He raised his brow. "I can sell you some bullets," he said, reaching into his stall. "That's a Z91, right? Hold on."

The shift in his tone took me by surprise. He'd gone from

petrified to professional in ten seconds flat. "Yeah, think you can handle that?"

"Of course," he said. "I'll sell you a few magazines if you can transfer the money." He showed me a credit pad.

Another burst of gunfire struck the car beside me. "Okay! How much for two magazines?"

He pursed his mouth. "Let's say, five hundred each."

"Five hundred credits? Are you serious? The sign over there says you have the cheapest prices in the sector."

"What can I say?" He grinned. "Demand has skyrocketed."

I started to tell him to toss the mags, but stopped myself. Why was I only going for more ammo when I had an arms dealer right in front of me? "What else you got?" I asked.

He gave me a sly smile. "What do you want?"

"How about some grenades?"

He stuck a hand inside his stall and brought out a small box. "Whatever you want, sir. Eight hundred creds for two."

I tapped my ear. "Siggy transfer one thousand, eight hundred credits to the asshole arms dealer named…" I paused. "Hey, jackass, what's your name?"

"Garin Shill," he said.

Even the fucker's name sounded sleezy.

Garin watched his pad for clarification, grinning once the transfer came through. "There it is!" he said, and tossed the first magazine to me. "Happy doing business with you, friend!"

"Yeah, yeah," I muttered, catching and sliding the bullets into my pistol. "Damn crook."

He followed with the second magazine, which I stowed in my belt for now, and finally the grenades.

"Move forward!" I heard a man's voice yell. "He has to be out by now!"

I smirked. "Not anymore."

* * *

By the time I had the second magazine inserted, I still hadn't made any progress. The Sarkonian soldiers were keeping their distance, refusing to let me get clear of this spot. I wondered how much more this vehicle could take before a bullet managed to tear its way through and into my flesh.

I eased up along the front of the car, trying to aim, but another shot hit the hood, forcing me down. "Give up, Renegade!" yelled a familiar voice.

That sounds like that Mercer woman, I thought. "I see you're awake!" I yelled back.

"Don't think you'll get away with that!"

I took a breath, glancing at the exit. It was only a dozen yards from here, but the corridor went on for a bit before the first turn. I might get shot in the back if I tried, but I couldn't wait here to get caught.

I shot at the group again. I didn't wait to see the damage, but

I knew I'd struck one guy in the waist and another in the crotch. Not a bad combo.

"That's enough, Captain Hughes!" barked Mercer. "I don't want to kill you, but I will if I have to!"

"I think you might have to, because I'm not letting you collect that bounty!" I yelled.

The merchant was still bunkered down at his shop, watching me. I wondered how long he'd wait before the money was no longer worth it.

"Hey, asshole, gimme something bigger!" I yelled. "I need a fucking army!"

"You'll want the black-label merchandise, then," said Garin. He reached under his shirt for a small locket, then swept it across the stall's side. The wall slid open, revealing a hidden compartment.

"What the fuck is that?" I asked.

He grinned, opening it. "Ever heard of a Howlizter 47?"

My eyes widened. "No way," I muttered.

He pulled the gun out of the box—a small enough weapon that you could trick the untrained eye into thinking it was nothing more than a pistol, but I knew what a Howlizter looked like. The three-centimeter grip housing the micro-generator gave it away, along with the silver-lined trim surrounding it. "Catch!" he yelled, tossing the gun in the air, high above our heads.

I caught it, tossing my own pistol to my other hand in the

process. The weight felt good as I wrapped my fingers around the tiny death cannon.

"You'll want to prime the generator by pressing that red button next to the trigger," said Garin.

I ran my index finger along the side, finding it. "There we go," I said, pressing it.

The gun hummed gently in my palm. "Purs like a dream, doesn't she?" asked Garin.

"Last chance, Hughes!" yelled Mercer.

I looked at Garin. "Better keep your head down!" I told him, then set my finger on the trigger and turned with my arm extended, taking aim at the small army.

I squeezed it, and a beam of red energy exploded from the barrel of the cannon, cutting through the nearby vehicles, slicing a line straight through their tops. Glass shattered in six cars instantly as my hand swept across the battlefield.

The Sarkonians dived out of the way, avoiding the beam as it moved across the place their heads had been. One was too slow, and the hot light cut through his wrist, slicing his hand clean off, along with the rifle he'd been holding. He screamed in a panic.

The laser stopped after a few seconds. I turned to look at Garin, who gave me a shrug. "It's only good for one shot," he told me.

"You mother fuck—"

Gunfire broke up my sentence as the soldiers got back on

their feet. Mercer shouted something I couldn't understand, and then she motioned to one of the soldiers, who handed her something.

She threw them in my direction, but they landed closer to Garin, rolling a few meters closer to him.

"Oh, shit," I said. "Grenades! Get out of—"

The explosion threw me back against the vehicle beside me, and I felt a wave of heat as I shielded my face. When I took my arm down, I saw a hole where the stall used to be.

Goddammit, Garin.

A figure appeared from the exit tunnel, but they were hard to make out through the grenade smoke. "Jace?! Where are you?"

"Who is that?" I asked.

As the smoke lifted, I saw Abigail standing in the tunnel, looking in my direction. She was holding something.

Something big.

"Abby? What the fuck are you...is that what I think it is?!" I shouted.

She didn't answer. Not with words, anyway. Instead, I got my confirmation when she propped up the massive quad cannon in her arms and fired an explosive shot toward the Sarkonians. The blast sent her flying back, into the hover cart she'd used to carry the other half of the equipment.

The bomb hit the ground between me and the military, shattering the concrete and sending multiple vehicles into the nearby buildings.

The entire dome echoed with thunder. My ears rang so loud I wasn't sure I'd ever be able to hear again. Before I could get back on my feet, I felt Abigail's hands on my wrist, pulling me up. "Come on!" she yelled into my face.

I blinked a few times, dragging myself up. Before I knew it, I was running behind her, passing by the quad cannon. "Wait!" I shouted. "I need this!"

I grabbed hold of it and lifted it onto the floating cart, pushing the bulky cannon through the hall. Abigail got beside me and helped.

When we made the turn at the end of the corridor, heading toward the open hangar, Abigail turned to me and said, "You could at least say thank you!"

"And give you the satisfaction?" I asked, still screaming over the ringing in my ears. "I'd never live it down!"

* * *

The airlock closed and I ran to the bridge, ready to give the order to leave, when I heard Freddie's voice. "Someone's outside!"

"Of course they are!" I returned. "We've got Sarkonians after us!"

"No, it's not a soldier," he said.

Hitchens ran to the window. "He's right! It appears to be a young girl."

"A girl?" asked Bolin, who was sitting on the couch. Octavia was in the process of bandaging his back shoulder, but he pushed himself up. "What does she look like?"

"It's Camilla," said Abigail. "Quickly, Sigmond, open the door!"

"Understood," said the A.I.

I looked outside to see the preteen running to the airlock, and shrugged. "Get her inside if you want. I'm getting us out of here in two minutes!"

I hustled to the cockpit, fastening my harness as soon as I was in the chair. "Siggy, tell me the second we're ready for lift-off."

"Acknowledged," he answered. Roughly ten seconds later, he followed it with, "All systems are ready for take-off."

"Is the girl onboard?" I asked. "Camilla."

"She just entered," Siggy informed me. "Closing the airlock now."

"Good," I said, flipping the ignition switch. We lifted off the ground, hovering momentarily, and then blasted forward in a damn hurry, breaking half-a-dozen flight laws in the process.

Several of the nearby ships wavered in place, but none took any serious damage. In a few short seconds, we were clear of the moon.

"Any pursuing ships?" I asked, quickly.

"None so far," said Sigmond.

I breathed a sigh of relief. "Let's get gone," I said, leaning back in my seat. "I think I've had my fill of people for today."

EIGHT

Bolin was in tears, hugging his little girl when I came back into the lounge. His hand was still wrapped and bleeding, but he barely seemed to notice. All his focus was on his daughter.

"Papa, I'm okay," she said, her voice muffled as he squeezed her.

"My little girl!" he cried.

"You're both safe now," said Abigail. "That's what matters."

"Everyone good?" I asked, looking at each of them. No one, aside from Bolin, appeared to have any injuries.

I also spotted Lex next to Octavia, watching the entire scene, a curious look on her face.

"Thank you so much for getting us out of there," said Bolin, turning to me. He had wide eyes and his cheeks were red from all the crying.

"We're cloaked and on the move," I explained. "The tunnel isn't far. We were headed to a space station, not far from here. If you want, you can find an outbound ship to take you away from the border. I'd recommend getting as far from Sarkonian space as possible. I'm sure you're wanted fugitives by now."

The girl looked at her father. "What are we going to do now?"

"I don't know, Camilla. I suppose we'll have to start over."

She frowned, sniffling. "I didn't mean to get you in trouble, Papa."

"It's not your fault. I never should have gone to that awful place."

It actually is her fault, since she stole that box in her arm, I thought, but kept my mouth shut.

"We should have left the second we arrived. I was a fool to think it had what we needed," said Bolin.

"Which was, what, exactly?" I asked.

They both looked at me.

I decided to clarify. "What did you go to that moon for?"

"Opportunity," said Bolin. "I wanted a fresh start. We both did."

"A fresh start from what?" asked Octavia.

"The Sarkonian Empire invaded our system," explained Bolin. "The occupation forced people to leave, and now most are scattered across the system. The new government began offering work a few months later, so I took one." He shook his head. "I didn't want to, but it was the only job I could find."

"I get it," I said. "Gotta do what you can to survive."

"Exactly. The Sarkonians won't let you leave their territory once they consider you a citizen, so I could only take what I found.

This was the best option." He dropped his head. "Gods, listen to me."

"It's okay, Bolin. You did the best you could," said Freddie.

"I almost lost my daughter today," he muttered. "I'll never forgive myself."

"But you didn't lose her," I said.

"No thanks to me," he answered. "It was you, sir. You saved her."

I fanned my hand at him. "She saved herself."

I returned to the front of the ship right as we approached the next tunnel. A rift formed and we went in, leaving the colony behind and, with any luck, the Sarkonians with it.

* * *

I gave Camilla my room while Bolin slept on the couch. It was fine, since I preferred to stay at the helm. Our flight time through the tunnel was short, so all I could afford was a nap. It would have been a decent one if Hitchens hadn't come knocking, interrupting me.

"Sorry to bother you," he said, stepping into the cockpit. He was entirely too fat to be here, but I didn't say anything.

"What is it?" I asked, hoping to cut through the small talk.

"With everything happening, I was never able to follow up with you."

I wiped my eyes. "I don't know what you're talking about."

"Back in the lounge, when Lex and I were opening that box. I asked if I could speak with you about something. It was actually rather urgent, but the situation escalated and—"

I held up a hand. "I get it."

He nodded. "Right, of course," he said, continuing. "It's about the star chart and our current heading."

"Oh?" I asked. "You find a better route?"

"Not quite," he answered. "I was studying the chart with Lex and comparing it to the galactic net's universal starchart. Granted, there are many unexplored regions, but it seems our end destination has already been explored and no planets were found."

"You mean the map leads to nothing?" I asked.

This was just great. I was a wanted fugitive in two empires without much money and hardly any supplies, and for what?

"Oh, no, Captain, that's not what I was saying. There's definitely something there. It simply isn't Earth."

"You're not helping your case, Hitchens. Just tell me what it is."

"In short, a planet, but nothing like what we're after. I believe, rather, this to be a second step along the path. I suspect the atlas is leading us to the beginning of the next leg of our journey."

"Next leg? You think this atlas of ours is only the first half or something?"

"That could certainly be the case. I wish I could say I knew."

He scratched the side of his face. "In any case, we must continue to follow the map. I'm certain we'll find an answer if we remain vigilant."

"Not like we got a choice," I muttered. "We can't go back."

"No, I don't suppose we can," he said, shaking his head. "But at least we can keep moving forward."

* * *

The slip tunnel took us into a system right outside a nebula. There was a bustling space station here, which happened to be just outside of Sarkonian territory. According to the galnet, the station was owned by a scientific research organization that paid a healthy tax to the Sarkonians to allow them access to this region.

Seemed like a waste of money to me, but what did I know?

"There are three ships with Deadlands identifiers," informed Sigmond.

"Put me through to the one with the cleanest record," I said.

A few seconds later, I was chatting with a guy named Hutch about taking two passengers into safer space. He agreed to a modest payment of four hundred credits and a bit of manual labor while onboard, and I told him that was fair. I knew Bolin would do whatever he had to in order to get his daughter to safety. If that meant cleaning some dishes and mopping a few floors for a week or two, I figured he could handle it.

I docked *The Star* with the science station, but didn't plan to stay very long. The encounter on our last stop still had me looking over my shoulder for the Sarkonians, which wasn't a feeling I enjoyed. The faster we left, the sooner I'd be satisfied.

Of course, our path had us heading directly into Sarkonian space again, which wasn't exactly ideal, but slipspace tunnels weren't flexible. They only ran through specific paths and ultimately didn't give a damn what you wanted. Our next tunnel, if we still planned on moving forward, remained our only option.

Once I had the ship docked, I opened the airlock and told everyone to get out and stretch. "Grab a drink if you're thirsty. Get some food. We lost our supplies in the city, so this is the place to pick up what you can."

"What about us?" asked Bolin.

"I've already found a ship willing to take you," I said.

He looked surprised. "You did that for us? Thank you so much!"

"It was nothing. I just made a phone call. Go to docking platform three and ask for Hutch. He's the captain of that ship. It's a cargo transport that specializes in...what was it, Siggy?"

"The procurement and transfer of adult entertainment, including video, holographic, handheld devices, and artificial humanoid replicants," responded Sigmond.

"Oh, yeah," I said. "He transports exotic goods. Nothing to worry about."

The girl, Camilla, was standing a few meters from us, talking to Lex. Her father called her over, after a moment, and told her it was time to leave. "Already? I was hoping to stay."

"These people have done enough for us, Camilla. We need to take care of ourselves now," said Bolin.

She nodded, looking at me. "I kept the box," she finally said, and lifted it up. "I left it inside on the couch. You can have it for saving us."

"That's nice of you," I said.

"I just found it in that pit, and we would've sold it to you if those soldiers didn't come."

Bolin smiled, hugging his daughter. "She's a good one, my angel."

The kid was a thief, so not much of an angel, but I didn't argue with the man. If he wanted to believe she was an innocent do-gooder, then by all means, let him delude himself.

"Bolin, a word?" called Octavia. "I need to check those wounds before you go."

"Ah, yes, thank you!" said the former shopkeeper. He looked at me. "Thank you again, Captain."

He went quickly to Octavia, who waited patiently with a medkit in her lap. Hitchens was there to assist, as usual.

Camilla stayed next to me, her eyes still on me.

I glanced at her, wondering why she hadn't followed her father. "Why are you still here?" I asked.

She seemed to study me. "You're a Renegade, aren't you?"

I raised my eye. "Who told you about that? Was it Abigail?"

She shook her head. "I've heard of Renegades. You steal and do what you have to do to stay alive. You're like me."

"You ain't far off," I told her. "But you're also not close. You do what you have to because you have no choice. I do it because I like it."

"You like stealing?" she asked.

"Only under the right circumstances," I explained. "But yeah, I do, and I'm pretty damn good at it."

"I only did it to help my Papa," she said, glancing at her father. He had his shirt off next to Octavia, who seemed more than eager to touch his back and reapply his bandage. "He does everything for me."

"You're right, he does," I said. "You want to take care of him?"

She nodded.

"Then, stay out of trouble. Do what he tells you. Don't be like me, kid. It ain't good for your health."

She lowered her head, her face full of disappointment. I could tell she wanted more.

I let out a long sigh. "Look, kid, you're not bad at thieving, but you keep going about it the way you are, you'll wind up dead or in a cage. You gotta get some brains if you wanna stay ahead."

"Brains?"

"When I was your age, I got arrested for stealing some bread. This was back on Epsy and I lived on the streets. Once they let me out of juvy, I got set up with a parole officer. You want to know what he told me?"

"Something about being good and getting off drugs?" she asked.

"Nah," I said, fanning my hand. "He said if I wanted to stay out of trouble, I had to work on not getting caught."

"What? Your parole officer said that? Why?"

I smirked. "His name was Jesson. Not really your average parole officer, but he was a good guy and he taught me to steal."

"He taught you? But isn't that bad for a parole officer to do?"

"Not on Epsy. That place was bad news. You had to be smart to get through those streets. Jesson understood that. He didn't waste time teaching us how to be upstanding citizens, only how to survive. That's the trick to this galaxy, kid. You gotta learn how to keep yourself alive. Sometimes that means stealing a loaf of bread to feed yourself. Other times, maybe it means you gotta shoot someone. Either way, the point is survival. Jesson showed me what I was doing wrong, running in blind, not understanding the layout of a place. He taught me how to set a mark and follow them. Study them. That's your problem, kid. You didn't case that facility before you snuck in. Even if you think you did, you didn't do a good job, because those cameras picked you up and that's how they got you. That's how you got caught. You gotta know all the blind spots, all the cracks in the glass. Next time, plan it out better. Be better than the fools chasing you and you'll always come out ahead. More importantly, when everything finally does go to shit, have yourself a way out."

She nodded, slowly. "Blind spots. A way out. I think I get it."

"No, you don't," I said, patting her shoulder. "But maybe you will in a few years, once you've fucked up a few more times."

NINE

I made sure we didn't stay on the station for too long. I figured it would be better for survival if we kept moving.

Hitchens and Octavia returned with a cart full of machines. I had no idea what any of it was, but I figured if they went through the trouble, it must be worth it.

We still didn't fully understand what was going on with Lex, after all, and something told me it would do us well to figure it out.

I moved *The Renegade Star* towards a nearby gas giant, closer to the next slip tunnel. "We ready to go, Siggy?"

"Yes, sir. Activating the slipspace drive now."

I brought up the star chart, examining the data I'd pulled from the device Hitchens had given me. The entire galaxy came into view, and a thin golden line stretched from one system to another, somewhere far from here, towards the outer rim. It was out of known space, as far as I knew. I had a hard time believing Earth, if it even existed, was so far away.

But hell, this map had to lead somewhere. They usually did, from my experience. Maybe this was the flight path of an old research ship from two thousand years ago, back when this technology was in its prime. Maybe we could scrap what we found and sell it off. If this whole expedition fell apart, there was still a chance I'd walk away with something.

Shit, you had to stay optimistic, right?

A tear in space formed ahead of me, just above one of the gas giant's eighty-six moons.

"The tunnel is clear, sir. Shall I proceed?"

"How long are we looking at this time?" I asked.

"Fifteen hours, approximately."

"Long enough for whiskey and regrets," I said. "Take us in, Siggy."

"Proceeding, sir."

The ship shuddered as our thrusters ignited, followed by a loud *SNAP*.

My seat jerked.

The Foxy Stardust on my dash bobbled violently.

"Sir, I am detecting unusual activity along the outer hull," said Sigmond.

The Renegade Star rattled again, this time so much that I felt my body slam into the harness around my shoulder. "Is that a fact?" I snapped. "Stop moving and scan the ship. Find out if we were hit by some kind of debris."

I activated the ship's com. "Attention, we're experiencing some turbulence. Sit your asses down and buckle up."

"Captain Hughes!" screamed a voice from the lounge. "You need to get out here now!"

I unbuckled my harness. "I swear to gods, Siggy, if you ran us into an asteroid, I'm going to kick your digital ass."

"I pray that isn't the case, sir."

The cockpit door slid open and I stepped into the lounge. Abigail was standing near the window, staring with a wide-eyed expression. She turned to look at me, open-mouthed. "We have a problem!"

"What are you—"

The airlock blew open with a shattering blast that knocked both Abigail and I on our asses. I hit the wall, rolling to the floor as the world blurred into a haze.

I felt a ringing in my ears as I struggled to stand, only to fall back against the wall. I could hear the faint screams of someone far away...or were they close? Was it Abby? Was she calling me?

I pushed myself off the floor, trying to see ahead of me. The blurred outline of something, a person moving, came toward me.

I reached for my pistol, thumbing the holster on my hip as I tried to get my grip, but it was difficult.

"...alert..."

A voice in my ear. It sounded like Sigmond.

"...sir, there is...you must...alert..."

"Siggy," I muttered, suddenly aware of how dry my throat was. "Siggy, what's going on?"

"The ship is being boarded, sir. You need to stand up, quickly."

"Boarded?" I muttered, coughing, but I couldn't see much of anything. Only the haze and black spots across my vision.

I sensed something moving. Figures coming out of the airlock. "Sir, you must get up at once. The enemy is here. You need to stand," said Sigmond.

One of them stopped, looking at me and walking closer. "What do we have here?" he asked in a deep, scruffy voice. "You must be the guy in charge."

"Who...the fuck...are you supposed to be?" I managed to ask, blinking rapidly, trying to make out his face, impossible as it was.

He laughed as he stood over me. "The man who's taking your ship."

Before I could say anything else, I felt the top of his boot slam into the side of my head.

* * *

A scream woke me.

"Get away from me!" yelled Octavia.

I cracked my eyes open to see her laying prone on the floor. Her chair was on its side, seemingly tossed to the other end of the lounge.

Two Union officers stood over her, each with a hand on a little girl's shoulder.

Lex.

There were too many things to process at once. Too many questions racing through my mind. I pushed every last one of them aside and focused on the girl in front of me.

She stood between them, helpless to do anything. Her cheeks were wet from crying as she watched them taunt the cripple on the floor.

Abigail sat behind her, across from me. I could see she was unconscious, knocked out in one of the chairs. Her head was drooping forward, bangs hanging across her forehead, hiding her eyes. Each of her wrists had been tied to the chair. Either she'd put up a fight or these guys knew exactly who they were dealing with.

I tried to lift my arm, but felt the pressure of a plastic strap across my wrist. *Fuck.*

"Please, you mustn't hurt the girl!" pleaded Hitchens. He was in the hall to the right of me, behind Octavia, an armed guard in front of him.

"Shut the fuck up, fat man!" barked the soldier. He pushed him, knocking the doctor to his knees. The other men laughed.

"Hey, I found another one!" called a voice. It came from the direction of the cargo bay.

Freddie. As the soldier brought him closer, I could see a mark across his left eye. It was fresh and still bleeding.

At least he tried to fight, I thought.

"Sit over here," the Union official in the center of the room said. A captain, by the look of him, the leader of this group.

I'll kill him first.

A young man approached the officer. He was lower ranking. Maybe an ensign in his mid-twenties. Black hair, well-kept. Quiet eyes. "Captain Anders, sir, what are your orders?"

The middle-aged officer looked over each of his new prisoners. Before his eyes could land on me, I pretended to be unconscious. "Extract what you can from their system. We'll blow the ship once we have what we need."

"The ship has an AI, sir. We won't be able to break its encryption with the equipment we have on hand," the young man responded. "If we were to tow the vessel back to Union territory, we could have a specialist meet us to assist in the extraction process."

The officer nodded. "We'll transfer these prisoners to the hold and return with both ships. Good catch on the AI, ensign."

"Thank you, sir," said the young man.

The captain looked at each of the other men. There were six in total, by my count. "Begin the transfer immediately. I'm ready to get out of this sector."

I cracked my eyes, barely enough to see anything. Two men took Lex by the wrists, pulling her away from the rest of us. She tried to resist. "No! Let me go!"

One of the men smacked her across the cheek. "Quiet down!"

She clutched the side of her face, but didn't cry.

"Stop it!" demanded Octavia. "She's just a child!"

"Tell her to calm down," ordered the captain.

Octavia looked at him, then at Lex, hesitating. "Lex, do as they say. I promise it will be all right."

Lex held her hands in front of her waist. "Okay, Octavia."

Another soldier cut the straps on Abigail's wrists, then lifted her legs. "Hey, help me with this one," he told another man.

"Sure thing," said the other soldier. Together, they hoisted the woman up and moved her to the airlock and into the other ship.

Hitchens and Freddie followed, each with a rifle buried in their backside. They said nothing as they walked.

Finally, only the captain, Octavia, and the ensign remained. "Let's get this woman onto the ship," said the officer.

"Are you going to carry me?" she asked him.

He raised his brow at her. "If we give you back that chair, will you play nice?"

"Are you that afraid of a crippled archeologist?" she asked. "What am I going to do against six armed soldiers?"

"Fine, but I promise you, if I see you try anything, I'll have this one—" He pointed to the ensign. "—shoot you on the spot, right in your little chair. Is that understood?"

She nodded.

"Ensign, if you would," said the captain.

The young man brought the chair over to her, then helped Octavia into it. "Hands where I can see them, please," he told her.

She kept them in her lap, and he began pushing the chair

towards the airlock.

I shut my eyes again, waiting. The captain approached me, standing there. I could hear him breathing.

"Now, what to do with you?" he muttered.

I heard a click in my ear. "Standing by, sir."

Good, but I couldn't give Siggy any orders yet. Not until I got myself out of this chair.

I felt a hand on my wrist as the officer began to untie me. It was taking him longer than it should, but that was because he only had one free hand to do it with. The other, I knew, was still holding his handgun. Without opening my eyes, I understood that the barrel was aimed squarely at my head. If I tried anything now, I'd be dead before I could move.

He managed to loosen the knot, and then got to work on the other, pushing my arm back in the process.

I let my body go limp, like a ragdoll. I fell forward.

The captain backed up, standing over me. I could sense the debate going on in his idiotic brain. Should he carry me or get one of his men to do it?

"Docker, get in here and load their captain up," he barked.

I nearly smiled at how predictable he was.

Docker came running from the other ship. "Yes, sir. I'll handle it."

"Hurry up and get him inside. We need to get out of this sector, quickly."

"But we have the cloak," said Docker.

"It only covers our ship," said Captain Anders. "And without access to this ship's system, we won't be able to use theirs."

"Does that mean we'll be vulnerable to attack?" asked Docker.

"Only if we stay here for too long. This area is too far out from Union space. There are ravagers, pirates, Sarkonians. We can't risk a fight while we have this vessel in tow."

"Understood, sir," said Docker, lifting my arm over his shoulder.

He pulled me to my feet, but I sank back to the floor, hitting it with a loud thud.

"Docker, you need to hold him up," said the officer.

"Right," said Docker. He bent down to take my hand.

I cracked my eye open, glancing at his waist...at the gun on his hip. It was an M-7, standard military issue. No fingerprint scanner on that one, unlike the M-8. Lucky for me.

As he lifted me, I felt my toes touch the floor. I was a foot taller than this asshole, so he strained to hold me. Good. That left him distracted.

It left him vulnerable.

My right arm swung across his chest and waist as he angled my body against his own, and my hand came within a few centimeters of his holster. Now was my chance.

I grabbed for the pistol at his waist and pulled it free. I opened my eyes fully, staring him in the face.

His mouth dropped as I met his gaze, and I dug the gun into his side. "Sorry, Docker," I said.

With our eyes locked, I pulled the trigger.

He collapsed on the floor in front of me and clutched his side.

I turned the weapon on the officer right as he was about to do the same to me. "Freeze."

He paused, hand around the grip of his gun. He glanced at his weapon, then at me.

"Go ahead," I muttered. "If you think you're fast enough."

Anders swallowed. "Your people are on my ship. If you try anything, they'll all die."

"But you'll die first," I said. "Put the gun down and step away. If you don't—"

He brought his arm up, suddenly, trying to catch me off-guard.

I shot him in the neck, forcing a hole clear through the other side. He looked surprised as he staggered back, falling on his ass, with blood pouring out of the new hole like an upturned soda bottle.

I stole the gun out of his hand, stepping back with it.

Anders gasped, with garbled, wet sounds instead of words, struggling to breathe. He clutched at the wall behind him, trying to pull himself up, but couldn't do it. All the strength in him was leaving. He'd be dead within the minute.

Good.

"Siggy, can you seal their docking clamps?" I asked. "We can't have these assholes trying to run."

"Their ship has its own AI unit, but I've been working to override its firewall. It appears to be missing the latest firmware update, which is good news. I should have access within the next ten minutes, approximately."

I heard someone yell from the other ship. "Hurry! Get to the captain!"

"Do what you have to, Siggy," I said. I glanced at Anders right as his eyes had gone empty and he stopped moving.

I stepped over Docker, who was fading in and out of consciousness, and ran to the wall adjacent to the airlock. Footsteps raced through the corridor on the other side.

Any second now.

I felt the wall behind me shake as the remaining soldiers came running. I could hear them grunting, clumsily stomping. Union dogs were never light on their feet.

I took a long, clean breath, my fingers on the triggers, extended my arms and turned into the airlock door.

Two men met my guns the very next second, and four eyes stared down the barrels.

They each started to open their mouths, but I fired a pair of bullets before either could make a sound.

Brains spattered across the wall behind them, and the bodies collapsed.

Four down, two to go.

I moved quickly through the interior of the ship. It wasn't like any Union vessel I'd ever seen. The design was newer, cleaner, more concise. Good for a small crew like this.

"Sir, if you'll pardon the interruption," said Sigmond. "I've infiltrated the firewall. The opposing artificial intelligence is attempting to stall my progress, but I believe I will take control—" He paused. "—Now."

I heard a mechanical sound beneath my feet, like something snapping into place.

"Locks have been secured. I will proceed with quarantining the other AI."

"Good luck," I whispered, getting close to a larger room in the center of the ship. It resembled my lounge, from what I could tell. An open area with tables and chairs, but the furniture was nicer and it lacked the same homely smell as *The Star*.

I heard a woman's voice from further down the hall. "Where am I?! Who are you?!"

"Guess Abby's awake," I said, turning my attention to the end of the corridor.

I took a few steps in that direction, but stopped when I heard a rustling noise, followed by a man's cry.

I raced toward it, prepared to fire, when I saw Abigail step into the hall, a rifle in her arms. She reacted by jerking the gun up toward me. "Whoa!" I snapped, raising my hands.

She pulled the gun away when she saw me. "Captain Hughes!"

"You okay, Abby?" I asked, staring at the barrel.

She turned the gun away from me, but didn't lower it. Smart, since there was still one more soldier to deal with. "What happened? I woke up a minute ago to this jackass trying to handle my—" She paused. "Where's Lex?"

"They have her somewhere on this ship." I tapped my ear. "Siggy, do you have eyes in here yet?"

"I do now, sir," he responded. "Everyone is being held inside the brig, near the back of the ship, opposite the bridge. You'll want to take the next right."

"Siggy says they're down that way," I said, pointing to the branching corridor.

"How many soldiers are left?" she asked.

"Siggy, what's the count? Is it just one?"

"Affirmative, sir."

"Just the one," I told her.

She nodded. "Follow my lead, then."

"You follow mine," I said, stepping in front of her. "Don't be thinkin' you're in charge just because you whooped that guy's ass."

TEN

I knew by the body count, up to now, that the last remaining soldier was the ensign, the mid-twenties kid who suggested they take our ship. I wagered a punk like that couldn't match me in a fight, especially with this crazy nun by my side, but I also wasn't stupid enough to drop my guard.

I raised both pistols as we neared the brig door. "I'm detecting movement inside," Sigmond said in my ear.

A quick nod to Abigail told her as much as she needed to know, that this was the right spot. She returned the action, extending her rifle.

"Open it, Siggy," I whispered, not wanting to touch the access panel. It was better to keep my weapons pointed ahead of me and my eyes forward.

"Right away, sir."

The door slid open, revealing the inside of the brig, and—

"I surrender!" said the ensign on his knees with his hands behind his head.

I kept my guns trained on him, then leaned inside to make sure there was no one else. Even with Sigmond's assurances about the crew count, it was better to be safe than dead.

After I was satisfied, I turned back to the man before me. "Huh," I muttered. "Didn't think he'd just give up."

Abigail rushed by me and kicked the boy in the chest. He let out a sharp woof as the air left him and he fell on his back. A second later, Abby had her knee on his ribs and a rifle in his mouth. "Where is she?"

"O-er d-er," he said, his tongue flapping against the metal.

"What's he saying?" I asked.

The ensign pointed to his left, across the room.

I walked past the two of them.

"Captain Hughes!" exclaimed Freddie. He was inside a small cell with Hitchens, some distance down the hall.

"Thank goodness!" said the doctor.

Across from them, I spotted Octavia in her wheelchair, with little Lex beside her on the floor.

"Everyone okay?" I asked.

"As good as can be expected," said Octavia.

I called back down the hall at Abigail. "Hey, before you kill him, can you ask that guy how to open these?"

"Answer," she commanded, squeezing the grip of the rifle.

"Might wanna take that gun out of his mouth first," I added.

She growled, but did as I said.

"The access code is 33918," said the ensign. "Please, don't shoot me!"

"This guy makes it too easy," I muttered.

I typed in the code on Freddie's cell. As soon as I hit the last digit, the door unlocked.

Freddie grabbed the bars and pushed it free. "Where are the rest of those men?" he asked.

"Dead or dying," I said, typing the code into Octavia's side.

Another click, but this time I grabbed the handle and pulled it myself. "Need someone to push you?" I asked her.

She rolled her wheels, moving towards the opening. "I have it, thank you."

Lex stood beside the wall, watching us as we gathered. "Kid, you can come out," I said. "It's safe now."

"It was safe before," she responded. "They came anyway."

"And if we don't get out of here, they'll come again with a different ship," I said.

"Jace!" snapped Abigail.

"Well, it's true," I said. "We need to get the hell off this Union ship and as far from it as possible."

"What about the boy?" asked Hitchens. "You don't plan to kill him, do you?"

"Why not?" I asked.

"W-Well, he's just a child, practically."

"Old enough to join the Union," I said. "Old enough to die for them."

"I don't care about the Union," the ensign said. "I swear, I'm nobody. I'm fresh out of training!"

"We can't just let you go, pal. You've seen too much," I said.

"Captain, couldn't we use the space in the cargo bay?" asked Freddie.

"What space?" I asked.

"I assume he means the spot behind the wall, where you stowed us during the ordeal with that Fratley person," said Hitchens.

"Oh," I said, knowing exactly what he meant, but not wanting to say it. The last thing I needed was another mouth to feed, especially a prisoner.

"If we take him, we might be able to get some intelligence out of him," suggested Freddie.

"Intelligence?" I asked. "He's a kid. He doesn't know shit."

"I-I can tell you how we followed you," he said, quickly.

"How's that, now?" I asked, waving my pistol at him.

He followed the barrel with his eyes. "Didn't you notice how fast we docked with you?"

I paused. "What do you mean?"

Abigail touched the rifle to his forehead. "Please, continue."

"The cloak," he answered. "We have a sixth-generation cloak. It's the latest in a new line, issued only to a handful of ships."

Sixth generation? I thought. I took a step closer to him. "You're lying."

"I'm not," he returned. "They upgraded us to it last month. It allows us the ability to travel through slipspace without decloaking. I swear, I'm telling you the truth."

"Through slipspace?" asked Hitchens.

I approached him. "Are you telling me you can cloak inside slipspace?"

"Yes, yes," he said, quickly. "We were cloaked when we followed you through the tunnel. We were tracking you before that, ever since you left the hospital."

Sigmond spoke through the com in my ear. "That matches my observations, sir. I believe he is telling the truth."

So, that's why the tunnel hadn't closed behind us. We were being followed, only we couldn't see the ship. I knew it had to be something. Tunnels never stayed open for that long without something coming through.

"What do you think, Captain?" asked Octavia.

"I believe him," said Freddie.

"So do I," agreed Hitchens.

Octavia motioned at him. "We should take him with us for now, maybe interrogate him later. If nothing else, we could use him as a hostage."

"Agreed," said Hitchens.

"Since everyone's chiming in with opinions, what are yours, Abby?" I asked.

She stared down at the ensign, a look of quiet hate in her eyes. "You and the others keep coming for us," she said in a steady tone.

"How many times has it been?"

"I promise, I had nothing to do with that," he answered.

"You're here now," she said.

He didn't answer.

Abigail's hands were tight around the grip of the rifle. Her eyes were fixed, unblinking, staring at the man in front of her. I'd seen that look a hundred times. The gears were turning in her head as she slowly convinced herself what she had to do...to pull that trigger.

"Abby," came a soft voice from behind the others. It was Lex, standing beside the cell door.

The nun blinked, loosening her grip. She turned around to look at Lex.

"I wanna go," said the little girl. "Can we please?"

Abigail looked down at the man, the debate raging in her brain. "Lex has the right idea," said Freddie. "Let's get back to the ship."

After a moment, Abigail eased back, off the chest of the ensign. She said nothing, getting to her feet. Lex took her hand and together they walked out of the brig.

I took the ensign by his shirt and yanked him onto his feet. "Kid says you get to live," I told him. "Guess it's your lucky day."

ELEVEN

"Are you sure about this?" asked Octavia, looking up at me.

"I've never been more certain of anything in my entire life," I said.

I wrapped my arms around the coffeemaker and lifted it with all my strength, there in the center lobby of the Union ship.

"If you say so, but I don't like the idea of moving anything from this ship onto ours."

"Oh, it's our ship, is it?" I asked, trying to look at her from behind the massive machine.

"You know what I mean," she said.

"Listen, lady, as the Captain of *our* ship, it's my decision, and I'm deciding that this beautiful piece of technology is essential to the job."

I began waddling toward the exit, trying not to drop it.

Octavia grabbed her wheels. "Whatever you say," she said, rolling close behind me. "How long before we leave?"

"As soon as I get this where it belongs," I said as I drew nearer to the airlock. "Freddie! Where are you?"

"Over here, Captain!" He yelled from inside the ship. He came running a moment later.

"Help me with this," I ordered.

Freddie gripped the bottom of the device. "Oof!" he let out, clearly as surprised by the weight of it as I was.

"Hold her steady now," I said as the two of us edged our way through the two airlocks.

"You don't even know if the coffee is any good," said Octavia.

"It has to be. It's from a Union ship," I said.

We brought the coffeemaker over to an empty table, the same spot as the last one, and set it down. "Whew," wheezed Fred.

"Think you can figure this out on your own?" I asked.

He looked confused. "Huh?"

"Make me some coffee," I explained. "Can you handle it?"

"Oh, I, uh, I guess so." He glanced at the machine.

"Great," I said as I began jogging to the cargo bay. "Don't fuck it up!"

Abigail and Hitchens were downstairs when I arrived, standing together near the center of the bay, looking at the fake wall where we'd stuck our new prisoners.

Prisoners, because there were three of them: the ensign from the brig, the man Abigail had knocked out, who was still unconscious, and the wounded guy named Docker. Octavia had seen to his bandages, despite my reservations.

"Ah, Captain," said Hitchens. "Are we departing?"

"Right as usual, Hitch," I said, going down the steps.

Abigail still had the Union rifle resting across her chest. "We were just discussing how to best tend to these men," she said, motioning to the fake wall.

"I had Fred raid their food supply while we brought them in here, so they can eat on that," I said.

She nodded. "Until we figure out where to take them."

"About that, if I might make a suggestion," interjected Hitchens. "There is a binary star system, not far from here."

"That so?" I asked, not liking where this was going.

Hitchens tapped his chin. "Are there any ravagers or otherwise dangerous types roaming that area?"

"None that I know of," I said. "But if you're suggesting we go out of our way just to drop a few Union brats off, I'm not sure I care enough to do it. There has to be something on our way."

"I'm afraid there isn't," Hitchens said. "I've looked through the star chart and this is our best option."

We didn't have time for an argument, not while we were still tethered to a Union ship. "Let's get moving and worry about the logistics later. You said that binary system is nearby? How far are we talking?"

"Two slip tunnels, I believe. Combined, the trek would amount to one day's journey. The first tunnel is the same as our current heading, however, regardless of what you decide."

"Fine, we'll take the first and figure the rest out later," I said.

I wasn't interested in keeping these men on my ship, but the thought of going that far out of the way to drop them off seemed like a waste of resources and time. Why had I stopped myself from killing all three of them when I had the chance? They'd come on this ship, captured my crew, tried to take my home away from me. These assholes deserved to die.

So why hadn't I killed them? Why did I give Abigail or the albino a say in what I did and who I shot?

Had I lost my touch, somehow?

Or was I getting soft?

* * *

Siggy managed to quarantine the other A.I., preventing it from calling anyone. At the same time, set the ship's course for the nearby gas giant, where it would enter the atmosphere and, with any luck, never be seen again.

I couldn't say it was much of a loss. That was one less Union ship in the galaxy.

What concerned me more than anything, presently, were the men in our storage room. One way or another, I'd have to decide what to do with them.

But not before I took care of an important matter. "Freddie! Get your ass in here!"

I was in the lounge, staring at the recently-acquired coffeemaker.

"Captain, is that you?" called Freddie from inside one of the guest quarters.

He came running a second later. "Where's my coffee, Freddie? I thought I told you to make some."

"I tried, but the machine is complicated," he said. I watched him mess with the control panel, attempting to punch in a command. "Medium cup, two creamers, no sugar. See? It won't work."

I moved him aside. "You're doing it wrong."

"Was I?" he asked. "I suppose I'm not used to it."

I tried entering another string of orders into the machine, then pressed Enter. Nothing happened.

"Maybe it's broken," Freddie suggested.

"Already? We just got the damn thing. No way it needs fixing this soon."

"What do you suggest we—"

"Is something wrong in here?" asked Hitchens as he arrived from the cargo bay.

"We're trying to get this to work," I said, turning the machine around to get a peek behind it.

"Did you, by chance, procure it from the Union ship?" Hitchens asked.

I looked at him. "Where else would I get it?"

"Ah, I see. In that case, I believe you'll need to have your A.I. unit integrate with it."

"What are you going on about?" I asked.

"Everything on Union ships is tied into its A.I. unit, even smaller devices like this one," explained Hitchens.

I scoffed. "Why the hell didn't Octavia tell me about this when I dragged the damn thing over here?"

"She may have assumed you knew," Hitchens said.

Now that I thought about it, I'd heard from Ollie a few months ago that the Union was moving away from independent hardware, preferring to use a closed system on each of their ships. He'd been complaining at the time about how more and more of the Union tech he'd bought had to be reconfigured to work outside of their ships. I thought nothing of it at the time.

"Goddammit," I muttered. "Siggy, can you interface with this thing?"

"Attempting now," said the A.I. "Access granted."

"That was fast," I said.

"I do aim to please, sir."

I punched in the command again and stepped back.

A glorious smell filled the lounge, igniting my senses. I went for the cup as soon as the machine finished, pressing the rim of the cup to my lips, and sipping.

And then I spit it out.

"What the fuck!" I snapped, setting the cup down.

"Is it bad?" asked Freddie.

Hitchens grabbed a second mug and filled it, taking a short drink. "Oh, goodness," he said, scrunching his nose. "That is not good at all."

"Fucking Union," I cursed. "They can't even get coffee right!"

* * *

Docker's wound tore again and had to be sewn. Octavia managed it while Freddie and I held him down. We couldn't have him trying anything, not that I thought he would.

Still, I wasn't a fool. Abigail kept a rifle pointed at his skull, just to be safe.

His eyes stayed locked on the barrel the entire time. I couldn't say I blamed him, what with the anger in Abby's eyes. She was ruthless when she had to be, and when it came to protecting Lex, I knew she'd do anything.

"That should do it," said Octavia, relaxing back in her chair. "He needs to rest, though."

"That right, Docker?" I asked. "You need to rest?"

"Whatever you want!" he said, still looking at Abigail.

I leaned forward. "How about you answer a quick question for me?"

"Okay," he said, breathing heavily.

"Who sent you after us? What were your orders?"

"Our orders?"

"Don't play stupid, Docker. Next to your captain, who's dead now, by the way, you're the highest-ranking person in your crew. I'm sure you know why you're here. Better yet, who gave you the order in the first place?"

He gulped, a bead of sweat running down his fat neck. "Th-That would be General Brigham. He's—"

"Did you just say Brigham? The guy in charge of the *Galactic* something?"

"The *UFS Galactic Dawn*," he answered, nodding.

I stared into his terrified eyes, seeing if there was any truth in there. I wagered there was, given how much fear I saw in him. But he was smart. He knew how to stay alive, and right now the only way to do that was to tell me the truth.

I got to my feet and looked at Abigail. "Let's put him back with the other two."

She lowered her gun, but only slightly. "You're done asking questions?"

"For now," I said, glancing at Docker. "But the two of us are going to speak again, Docker. You got that? And I don't want any problems from you."

"No problems, sir," he said.

We tossed him in the cell and closed the wall, locking him inside with the other two prisoners, the ensign and the officer who'd tried to tie up Abigail. They had no light, no bathroom, nothing but the cold metal surrounding them on all sides. It was hardly a way to live, but certainly better than dying.

* * *

Abigail and I met in the cockpit, a few minutes later. She placed her rifle at the door. "What's going on?" she asked me.

I cut right to it. "Who the fuck is Brigham?" I asked. "Does he have some vendetta against you? Was he there when you kidnapped the kid?"

"Brigham? He's the head of the Union's Third Defense Operational Wing. He controls their largest carrier."

"A carrier," I repeated. "A ship that's so goddamn big it can fit a thousand of mine inside it. *That's* the guy chasing you." I paused, shaking my head. "The guy chasing *us*."

She nodded. "But he can't find our ship if we keep moving."

"We *were* moving, but these six idiots still managed to find us."

"I wasn't expecting that."

"You and me both. Siggy, can you pull up everything you have on General Brigham?"

"Right away, sir."

I leaned against the wall, pulling out a piece of hard candy and unwrapping it. Before tossing it back in my mouth, I glanced at Abigail, who seemed to be watching me. "You want one?" I asked, offering the sweet.

"Oh, I'm okay," she said, holding her palm up.

"Suit yourself," I said, throwing the candy back. It was a delicious kessil flavor, based on a fruit from Kandil Six. Common enough that you could find it on just about every planet in Union space as well as most Deadlands worlds. *Common for a reason*, I thought. They were easy to grow, simple to harvest. But more importantly, they were perfect for hangovers.

I had six sitting in the fridge. Maybe I'd go and grab two of them when this business was over, along with some soup. I ran out of tomato, but I still had a noodle and beef blend waiting for me in the cabinet. Now that I thought about it, I really needed to go grocery shopping.

Did they have grocers this far out in the Deadlands? I honestly didn't know.

"Analysis complete," said Siggy. "Please forgive the delay, sir. I had to mask our network ID before accessing the galactic net."

"No problem," I said, cracking the candy with my teeth. "Let's see this guy's bio."

A holographic display appeared over my console, showing the head and chest of a middle-aged man with white hair and brown eyes. The image, if I had to guess, probably came from his military record, since he wore a Union dress outfit, his chest fixed with a large block of ribbons. I couldn't guess what any of them were for, but if the biography was any indication, the man understood war better than most.

Name: General Marcus H. Brigham

Age: 62

Place of Birth: Androsia

Rank: General, Grade-2

Height: 182 cm

Marital Status: Divorced

Latest Assignment: UFS Galactic Dawn

-List of Medals and Awards-

I reached over and touched the list of awards. It expanded, revealing what must have been an additional fifty lines. There were several impressive-looking ones, although I had no idea whether they actually were.

Medal of Valor (on three occasions)

Norsdad Medal of Excellence

Legion of Honor

Galactic Cross

Union Medal of Excellence (on six occasions)

Union Fleet Decoration for Gallantry

Union Fleet Award for Valor

The rest of the list went on for several pages, dating back twenty-five years. This was a dedicated soldier if ever I'd seen one.

I collapsed the awards and brought up the model for his ship, the *UFS Galactic Dawn*. It took the place of Brigham in the holo display—a carrier with what must have been a thousand strike ships. There was probably enough firepower onboard this monstrosity to glass an entire city, maybe even a planet.

"What do you think?" Abigail asked, staring over my shoulder.

"I think we've got a problem," I said, stepping back from the display. "And it's worse than I expected."

TWELVE

"Where have you been?" asked Octavia as Abigail and I joined her in the cargo bay.

Hitchens was there beside her, each of them near the electron microscope. "In all the commotion, we nearly forgot to check in on the blood analysis," said the doctor.

"Did you find anything?" asked Abigail, passing me in a hurry.

I stayed back and observed, having learned a long time ago that sometimes it's better to shut up and listen.

Octavia retrieved a vial of blood from the table. "It's interesting, actually. Lex's—"

"Where is Lex?" asked Abigail. "I'd rather she not hear this."

"Frederick is looking after her," assured Hitchens. "I believe he's going over her spelling lesson."

Abigail nodded. "Thank you. What's wrong with her cells?"

"Actually, that's the strange part. There's nothing *necessarily* wrong with them. They're just...better. In fact, the more I examine Lex, that's the conclusion I keep drawing. She's simply *better*."

Abigail tilted her head. "I'm not sure I'm following."

"The human body is a funny thing. No matter the situation, it will try to heal itself, to survive as long as possible." She took her fingernail and slid it along her wrist. "When you get cut, there's damage, so it needs to be healed. You have to be put back together. Normally, we'd apply some medicine and it wouldn't be a problem, but out in the wild, your body has to do everything on its own. Scarring is how it does that."

I leaned forward, away from the wall. "Lex *didn't* scar, so what does that mean?"

"From what I can gather," continued Octavia, "which isn't much since I don't have access to a lab, Lex's body isn't creating a disorganized scaffolding for the cells to grow on. That's unusual, because if it were one of us, we'd see the opposite. Our cells would attempt to heal the wound, building that scaffolding in the process, and a scar would form. Instead, Lex's blood is creating a crystalline structure with clean regularity. This is beyond unusual. It simply doesn't happen."

"You got all that from testing her blood?" I asked.

"Partially. Her blood cells, unlike the rest of ours, contain no defective or inadequate copies. They grow orderly, making for flawless regeneration." She looked at the vial of blood in her hand. "They're perfect."

"Does any of this make sense to you?" I asked, looking at Abigail.

"A little," she said, giving me a nod. "Octavia, if I'm understanding you correctly, you're telling us that Lex's body can heal faster, is that right?"

It's not *just* that," said the former Union medical officer. "If these early screenings are right, her white blood cells are also far more *efficient*. For whatever reason, she was born like this."

"Could those Union scientists have done this?" I asked.

"As far as I know, the technology to genetically modify a human at this level does not exist, but the Union has its share of secrets and hidden labs, so who knows?"

"I took her from one, so clearly they were doing something to her," said Abigail. "I thought it was because of her tattoos, but what if..." Her voice trailed. "...what if there was more to it?"

Hitchens, who had been silent for most of the conversation, cleared his throat. "I believe we still have much to learn. As talented and brilliant as Octavia is, she isn't a biologist. None of this is certain, not without more evidence and testing."

Octavia nodded. "I agree. We'll need to find a proper facility with—"

"We don't have time for that," I interrupted. "We've got a Union ship the size of a small moon after us. Whatever this is," I motioned at the electron microscope and the vials of blood next to it. "We can figure it all out later, once we're in the clear."

"But what about Lex?" asked Abigail.

"You heard Octavia. Her health is fine. Better than fine, if I got it right."

"You did," confirmed Octavia.

"See? I'll admit, half of the science was lost on me, but I got the important shit."

Abigail took a step closer to me, staring at me with her green eyes. "Once we take care of the rest, I want your assurances that we'll find answers for Lex."

The tone in her voice was vulnerable, in a way, or about as close to vulnerable as a woman like this could be. It caught me off guard. "We'll do that," I said, staring at her.

"I have your word?" she asked, leaning in.

Her scent flowed across my face, like I was noticing it for the first time. Her blonde hair fell below her shoulders in a disorganized mess, but there was something to the madness, the way the light bounced off the strands. It was…

What the fuck am I doing?

I took a step back. "Yeah, all right, lady. You got it." I turned away from her. "If we're done talking about magic blood, I'm going to bed. Hitchens, make sure you feed the prisoners. Don't touch my fruit."

"Y-You want me to…to feed the three of them by myself?"

"Someone has to. Get Freddie to help you." I walked into the corridor, not giving him a chance to respond.

Thirteen

"...leaving slipspace, sir."

I cracked my eyes open, groggy and tired. Siggy's voice, calm as it was, felt like needles in my brain. The holo screen in my room was still on, illuminating the dark. When had I fallen asleep?

"Sir," said Sigmond. "We're about to—"

"Okay, I heard you," I said, turning on my side. All I wanted to do was go back to sleep. "Siggy, how long until—"

I froze when I felt it. The wet, cold liquid in my bed.

Had I pissed myself?

No, that wasn't it. It didn't smell like piss. I licked my chapped lips, tasting what remained of the whiskey in my mouth.

I swept my hand across the drenched sheet, to where the puddle was at its deepest, and felt the empty flask with my index finger. I must have fallen asleep drinking it.

I eased off the bed, drops of whiskey falling from my boxers. *I need a shower*, I thought.

The sheets would need to be changed. I'd have to clean the mattress, too. The last thing I remembered, I was in bed, watching an old holo film about a professional thief. He was trying to rob a bank, but I couldn't remember the ending.

It didn't matter. I'd spent longer than I meant to, and I still had to bathe and dress, all in the next few minutes. If Abigail saw me like this, she'd lose her mind.

Not that I cared. *Let her try to lecture me. Doesn't matter. This is my ship.*

I yawned and took a swig of water from the jug beneath my bed, then told Siggy to start up the shower, medium hot.

Eight and a half minutes later, I was clean and toweling my face. I stood in front of the mirror, examining my bloodshot eyes, thirsty as hell. *Maybe I should lay off the booze,* I thought, remembering how when I was twenty-five, I could drink my way through every bar in town and still be sober enough to take a woman home to bed.

In those days, back when I was just some punk kid on Epsy, I thought I could drink and fuck my way into eternity. No one would stand in my way. I was going to have it all and live forever.

But that was how it was when you were young and stupid. You thought the world was yours, and maybe it could've been, had you played a better hand, but kids are always too stupid to see it, to know what the right call is.

They fall in love, make silly choices. They kill the wrong guy or screw the wrong girl. That's how you end up dead in a gutter, a worthless little shit without a credit to your name, gone before anyone knew who you were.

Without a ship or a crew.

Without…

A knock at the door jarred me. I dabbed the towel on my neck and then wrapped it around my waist. "Who is it?"

"Lex!" said a mousy, muffled voice.

"What is it, kid?" I threw some pants on, grabbing my shirt.

"Open up!"

I groaned as I got my shoes on, then hit the control by the door.

She was standing there with a grin on her face, twisting left and right, with a foot off the floor. "Um, what are you doing?"

"Nothing. What do you want?" I asked.

"Um."

"Just say it," I told her.

"Can I have a, um," she looked at the floor. "Can I have a piece of candy?"

"Candy? Is that why you're here?" I pulled open my desk drawer and retrieved a few pieces of hard sweets. "Sure thing."

Her eyes lit up when she saw them. "You mean it?!"

I tossed one of them to her, bubblegum flavor. "Enjoy."

"Wow, thanks!" she unwrapped it as quickly as her little hands would allow.

I grabbed my holster and pistol, strapped them around my chest and waist, and made sure they were secure.

"Hey, Mr. Hughes," said Lex, the hard candy clicking against her teeth. "What's that smell?"

I glanced at the bed, which was soaked in whiskey. "Oh, uh, that's nothing. Don't worry about it."

She wrinkled her nose. "It smells bad. Did something break? What is it?"

"Nothing, kid. Hey, look here." I placed a second piece of candy on the table. "Here's another. Save it for later, or don't. Just take it and get out of here."

She snatched it up with a grin, burying it in her pocket. "Wow, thanks Mr. Hughes!"

I nudged her to move. "Time to go."

We both left the room and I made sure it was secured. "Where's everyone else?" I asked when we were in the lounge.

She bit on the candy. Clack clack clack. "Abby and Freddie are playing in the bay. They said I couldn't stay."

"What about Hitchens and Octavia?"

"They're in their room with the door locked," she said.

Oh boy, I thought. "Who's supposed to be watching you, then?"

"Abby said to sit in the lounge but it's boring here."

"So you thought you'd bug me, huh?"

"Yup!" She grinned.

I started walking to the cockpit, away from the couches and tables.

"Are you leaving?" she asked.

"I told you, I got work—"

"Me too!" she exclaimed, running after me, coming up to my side.

I glanced down at her, only to see a smile with a piece of red candy between her teeth. "Whatever. Do what you want," I said, not caring enough to stop her. "Siggy, what's the status of the ship? Are we almost out?"

"Arriving at the next slip gap point in less than two minutes, sir."

"As soon as we're out, activate the cloak," I ordered.

"Understood, sir."

"What's a cloak?" asked Lex, curiously.

I took my seat behind the dash. She did the same, sitting in the copilot chair to my right. "It protects the ship. Keeps us invisible."

"Is that so the bad guys don't find us?"

I chuckled. "Sure, kid. The bad guys." I almost told her the truth, that some folks considered me a bad guy. I thieved, killed, and smuggled my way across the galaxy, breaking every law I could in the process. Did that make me bad? Or did it make me a survivor?

Was there a difference?

"Are the people in the dark room bad?" she asked, after a moment.

It took me a second to realize who she was talking about. "Oh, you mean the soldiers, is that it?"

She nodded.

"They're bad," I said, and kept it at that.

Truth was, each of those guys might be all right. Maybe deep down, they had a solid moral compass. Who the hell really knew? But they'd come here with an aim to take this girl from us, to steal her away and deliver her to scientists. She had to see them as evil, for her own sake. Maybe then, she'd stay far away.

The tunnel began to open, a tear forming before us like a nail through cloth.

But instead of darkness on the other side, I was surprised to find a blinding light, forcing me to shield my eyes.

"What is that?" asked the little girl beside me.

"Siggy, analysis," I said, ignoring the question.

"It seems this tunnel ends near the inner orbit of a yellow star, classification number 392—"

"Decrease brightness on the screen by fifty percent."

"Acknowledged."

The screen dimmed immediately, allowing me to put my hand down, away from my eyes. "How close are we to that thing?"

"65 million kilometers, approximately," answered Sigmond.

I nearly cursed. The closest safe distance a ship like *The Renegade Star* could get to a star this size was 60 million kilometers. A little more and we might have taken some serious damage to the hull...or worse.

This was one terrible location for a tunnel to drop out.

"Give me the next location," I ordered. Coordinates appeared on my screen. It wasn't far. Good.

Another set lit up, surprising me. This one was on the opposite side of the star from our current position.

"Siggy, what is this?" I asked.

"I have sent the coordinates for each tunnel appropriate to our two destinations."

Two? Oh, right. I'd almost forgotten about the side trip Hitchens wanted to take. "Which one has us following the atlas?"

"The first coordinates," answered Sigmond.

I almost ordered the ship to continue on its present course, to follow the atlas, but in doing so, we'd be stuck with those three hostages, possibly indefinitely. I couldn't have that. Hitchens, for all his absurdity, had raised a good point.

"What are we doing?" asked Lex, now on her second piece of candy. Purple, by the look of it.

"I'm trying to decide where to go," I said.

"Which is the right way?" she asked.

"I don't know. That's the whole problem."

"Did you ask Abby? She always knows what to tell me when I don't know."

"No offense, kid, but that's the last thing I want to do right now." I could still feel the hangover weighing on me.

"Well, then you gotta decide," said Lex, cheerily.

"Kid, it isn't that simple—"

"Captain!" screamed a voice from the other side of cockpit door.

I turned in my seat the second I heard it.

"Captain Hughes!" It sounded like Freddie.

I scrambled to my feet and ran out into the lounge, leaving Lex in the cockpit. "What the hell are you screaming about?"

Freddie nearly collided with me as I entered the lounge. "Captain! We have a serious problem!"

"Spit it out, then," I snapped.

"The prisoners, the Union soldiers, they're out of their cell and they have Doctor Hitchens!"

"Stop!" called Octavia from down the hall.

"Fuck," I muttered, reaching for my pistol, unholstering it. I looked at Freddie. "Follow!"

We raced through the corridor toward the cargo bay. I came to a stop near the door, creeping up to the wall. I grabbed Freddie by his shirt and kept him back. "Wait!" I said in a loud whisper.

He nodded, but I could see the panic in his eyes. Beads of sweat streamed down his cheeks and forehead. The panic was beginning to set in.

I leaned closer to the edge of the door, trying to eye whatever the hell was going on in there.

I spotted Abigail first, standing a few meters in front of two of the men. One had Hitchens in a headlock. Docker, by the look of him. The other guy, the same one Abigail had knocked out on the other ship, had a broken piece of pipe in his hand. Part of me wondered where he could have gotten it, but I buried the thought, focusing on the situation.

Two men, one hostage, no sign of the third, I thought. *Abigail's close enough to strike, if I need it. Octavia has to be close, too, but the angle's no good. She might be under the overhang, beneath the stairs.*

Fuck, there wasn't enough information. I needed a better vantage point.

Fast, heavy breathing half-a-meter behind me. *Oh, and there's Freddie, I guess.*

"Let him go and I promise, we won't kill you," Abigail told the two Union soldiers.

"We just want off this ship!" said Docker, trying to keep Hitchens' head in front of his own. "We don't want to hurt anyone, but we will if we have to!"

"If you do," began Octavia. Her voice seemed to come from beside them, in a place I couldn't see. "You'll have given up your only hostage. Is that what you want?"

"We'll still have the two of you!" snapped the one whose name I didn't know.

"Wrong," corrected Abigail. "I'd kill you both before you could touch us."

He laughed. "You only got the drop on me the first time because I thought you were asleep. You won't get lucky again!"

"It wasn't luck," she said. "And I really was asleep. If I can do that, half-disorientated and with a beating headache, just imagine how I am now."

"Bullshit!" He raised the pipe. "You try anything, I'll go for the cripple first!"

I eased my way into the cargo bay's upper floor, putting my hand out to keep Freddie back. Slowly, I made my way to the back of the railing, overlooking the entire area.

Abigail noticed me right away, but only gave me a single glance. "Your friend in there had the right idea. You should stay in the cell like he did."

"He's just scared," said Docker.

"I'd call it smart," she answered. "The two of you...not so much."

She looked at me again, but only for a second. Long enough to get the message across. Long enough for a signal.

I aimed my barrel at the one with the pipe, and I pulled the trigger tight.

The bullet whizzed through the air, sniping him through the jaw, scattering blood and bone against the wall behind him.

He spun around like a doll, blinking rapidly, and then collapsed, releasing the pipe.

"Bennett!" screamed Docker.

"Was that his name?" I asked, stepping down the stairs.

"How did...where did you...!?"

"Let him go, Docker," I cautioned. "Or else."

"I…I…"

"We'll forget about this if you do what we ask," said Abigail.

"Do what they say, you idiot!" called the young ensign, who was still in the cell.

Octavia was close to his position, behind a few crates, like she'd been trapped there. "Listen to your friend!" she said.

"If I do, you won't kill me?" he asked.

"We might, if you try this again," I said.

Abigail looked at me with an expression that told me I should probably stop talking.

"We won't hurt you, Docker," said Abigail.

He nodded, and began to loosen his grip, but when Abigail started to move, he tightened it again. "Stop!"

She sighed. "Docker, what are you doing?"

"I bandaged your side, and this is how you repay me?" asked Octavia.

"Th-The situation is complicated!"

Just then, I spotted Freddie on the upper deck, climbing over the railing, three and a half meters from the bottom.

I turned my head, watching him. "What the f—"

Before I could finish, he was in the air, falling straight towards Docker. He landed on the man's shoulders, sending both of them, as well as Hitchens, onto the deck floor.

Abigail lunged forward, after Hitchens, while I went for

Docker. Freddie managed to roll, surprisingly, and got to his feet in seconds.

As Docker started to rise, I slammed the butt of my pistol into his nose, and he fell again. "Stay the fuck down, you idiot!"

FOURTEEN

I sat beside the open cell with the two men inside. Docker was on his knees with steel cuffs on his wrists and a gag in his mouth, while the ensign stood beside the entrance. "Smart move, not trying to escape. Smarter than your stupid friend back there."

"Nnfph," said Docker.

"Right," I agreed. "Very stupid."

The ensign nodded. "I knew there was nowhere to go."

"See? Smart. Now, stay that way and you'll get out of this in one piece."

"When?" he asked.

I was surprised by his calm, almost like he wasn't terrified, like he didn't really view me as the enemy. "Whenever I say. Just keep quiet and don't cause me any problems. Do that, and I'll drop you both off first chance I get."

"Do you have any idea where that will be?"

"Not yet, but the guy Docker had his arm around, Hitchens, he knows a place. Some habitable planet a short slip away."

"I understand," said the ensign. "And I'll make sure Docker doesn't try anything again."

"Good," I said. "You're smarter than you look, kid."

"Alphonse," he corrected.

"What?"

"That's my name. Ensign Alphonse Malloy."

His tone was different than before, back when we'd captured him. He was calmer, less frantic, like all the fear in him had drained. Did he think he was safer now, since he'd refused to join his crewmates' escape attempt, or was there more to it? I had assumed he'd stayed back out of fear, but looking at him now, I wondered if there was more to it.

"Okay, Alphonse," I said, giving him a dismissive wave. "Whatever. Just stay put and don't piss me off."

"I won't cause you any trouble."

"It's no trouble for me," I said, stepping back from the cell. "You're the one who'll end up dead."

* * *

I returned to the lounge, walking straight to the fridge. I was thirsty and still hung over, so the only solution was a piece of kessil. If I was right, I'd find four in the fridge.

I pulled the door open and bent down, looking on the third shelf. There was a bottle of mustard, two refrigerated dinners, and absolutely no kessil fruit.

"The hell?" I asked. "Hey!" I raised and turned my head. "Who took my fruit!"

I heard a slurping sound coming from the sofa. "Sowwy," said Lex, chewing on one of the kessil. She swallowed, then took another bite.

I glared at her. "Lex, what is that in your hand?"

"I dunno," she said, smiling, trying to play innocent.

I shut the fridge, burying the fury in my throat as it slowly rose to a killing rage. "Are you sure about that?"

She scrunched her chin into her shirt, soaking the rim with liquid from the fruit. "I dunno," she giggled.

I let out a long sigh, accepting my defeat at the hands of this child. "I'll be on the bridge."

"Can I come?" she asked, leaping off the sofa, the mostly eaten kessil still in her hand.

Without answering, I walked into the cockpit and shut the door behind me, locking it.

I collapsed into my seat and tried to get comfortable. I was exhausted and hungover, tired of dealing with all this bullshit. Maybe a nap in here would do me good, but only if everyone left me—

"Sir, I hate to intrude, but..."

Goddammit. "What is it now, Siggy? Have you come to betray me, too?"

"Heavens no, sir. I would never dream of such a thing. I simply wanted to inform you that you have yet to provide our next destination."

"Destination?" I asked.

"We need to choose a route. Do you not recall our last conversation? It was just before the interruption involving Mr. Frederick Shiggorath."

Oh, right, I thought. With all the insanity in the cargo bay, not to mention the *catastrophic* loss of my kessil, I'd completely forgotten about the two slip tunnels.

"Shall I continue forward, per our original path?" asked Sigmond.

"No, we're taking the other one. The one Hitchens gave us. The detour."

"Understood. Proceeding with new destination. Star system X1-20-5519."

"Sounds like a wonderful place with amazing people," I said.

"I wouldn't know, sir, but I should hope that it is."

"Me too, Siggy." I leaned back, propping my feet on the console and closing my eyes. "Me too."

* * *

The tunnel took six hours to cross. I slept through most of it. When I finally opened my eyes, I felt better than I had in days.

"Siggy," I muttered, licking my lips and wishing I had some water.

"Yes, sir?"

"The next time I'm drinking straight whiskey in the middle of the night, remind me how awful the last time was, would you?"

"Of course, sir."

I leaned forward, rubbing the grime from my eyes, and blinked, trying to focus. We'd just entered normal space again, having left the tunnel behind. According to the map, we were in the X1-20-5519 system. There was one planet, waiting in the goldilocks zone, three smaller planetoids in deep orbit, and a few hundred asteroids. Hardly the kind of place you'd want to visit, but it would do fine for unloading prisoners.

I entered a command to bring us closer to the planet, then set us in a stable orbit. "Cloak the ship," I ordered. "Hopefully, this doesn't take us long."

"Shall I begin landing procedures, sir?"

"Go ahead," I said, getting up from my chair. I tapped the Foxy Stardust bobblehead as I did, letting it bounce chaotically while I left the cockpit.

"Captain," said Freddie, who was sitting with Abigail. "Have you been on the bridge this whole time?"

"I had work that needed tending," I lied. "Are those two soldiers playing nice?"

"We fed them and left them in their cell," said Abigail. "They should still be alive in there."

"Either way, we're at the system Hitchens gave me, so we can finally get rid of them. You two think you can help me get them on the shuttle?"

"With pleasure," said Abigail.

"I'll be happy to help," said Freddie.

"I bet you would," I smirked. "Just don't jump on anyone this time, if you can help it."

He gave us an embarrassed smile. "I was only trying to help."

"And you did," said Abigail. "We'll have to work on your form, though. You could have broken something."

He nodded. "I'll do whatever you ask."

"Sounds like you're really taking to this whole training thing," I said, and I really did mean it. "Keep it up and you might actually learn how to fight."

He smiled. "Thank you, Captain."

* * *

We stepped out into the light of sun and saw the endless valley before us, a vibrant yellow field, interlaced with spots of green.

The Renegade Star had landed in the western part of the largest continent, twenty kilometers from the ocean. There was a freshwater river nearby, with two large lakes, ripe for drinking. According to the database, there had been a colony here, half a century ago, but no longer. Because of a border dispute between the Sarkonians and another group, the colony was uprooted and moved to a world called Hexios.

It seemed the Sarkonians had still yet to make use of this

place, but it would do just fine for our purposes. The wildlife was mostly safe, with a larger population of smaller critters than not, and there were wild orchards of fruit trees, remnants from when the settlers had been here.

"What do you think?" asked Abigail, standing beside me as I scanned the horizon.

"It's not a bad place," I said. "Should be good until we send someone to pick them up."

"About that," she went on. "What's your plan to get them rescued?"

"Siggy suggested an encrypted message to the Sarkonians, once we're clear of their territory. Since they're clearly working with the Union, they should have no problem rescuing them."

She nodded, taking a deep breath of air. I imagined it must feel nice, not being cramped inside a ship the size of mine for once. "Does it make you miss the Church?" I asked.

"What do you mean?" she asked, turning to look at me.

"Wide open spaces, fresh air, your two feet on the ground. Seems like a better alternative to living on *The Star*."

"I'm not complaining. Not at all. I'm sorry if I gave you the impression."

"No, I didn't think you were," I assured her. "I was just wondering."

"Were you?" she asked, giving me a warmer smile than I was used to seeing from her. "Interesting."

The look on her face gave me pause, and I cleared my throat. "Okay, I've seen enough. Let's head back."

"Already?" she asked, a disappointed tone in her voice.

"What? Did you want to go frolicking in the grass? Do you need time to play in the mud?"

She laughed. "Do I strike you as the frolicking type?"

"I'm not answering that," I said, walking back onto the ramp of the cargo bay.

I heard the footsteps running through the corridor on the second deck, growing louder by the second. "I wanna see!" demanded a tiny, eager voice. Lex darted into the cargo bay with her hands raised, looking like she was in a panic. "I wanna see the outside!"

"Whoa," I said as she zipped past me, nearly running into my leg. I dodged her, and she continued unabated towards the ramp and into the field.

Abigail laughed when she saw her, putting her hands on her hips as the little girl sprung off the metal grate and into the mud, stomping her feet around. "It's so pretty!"

"Great, now I'll have mud to deal with," I said, watching as she managed to get the wet dirt on her feet, knees, and hips, all within a matter of seconds.

Abigail laughed, and for a few seconds it looked almost natural on her.

I supposed it was nice to see the kid having fun for a change.

After everything she'd been through, maybe it wasn't so much to ask, just to play in the mud.

"Sir." Sigmond's voice popped into my ear, startling me.

"Something wrong, Siggy? Did the scans turn up anything?" I had asked him to continue searching the planet to look for anything Docker and Alphonse might find that could give them a means of escaping. I couldn't have them accidentally stumbling on a lost shuttle or a communications device. They needed to stay here until we were long gone.

"Not quite, sir. On the contrary, the scans revealed very little," he explained. "However, I am detecting another slipspace tunnel opening. It appears to be the same tunnel we used."

"Did someone follow us here?" I asked.

"That is unclear for the moment."

I looked back at Abigail and Lex. "Hey, you two! Get back in the ship!"

"Aw," groaned Lex. "Already?"

"I said *now*!"

She frowned, but did as I told her, running back and into the cargo bay, leaving a trail of mud in her path.

Abigail came jogging behind her. "What's going on?" she asked as she approached me.

"We have company," I said.

"Union or Sarkonian?" she asked.

"Does it matter? Either way, we need to get out of here."

She nodded, heading inside without another word.

I hit the control near the door, raising the lift. "Siggy, begin the ignition sequence."

I watched the gate close, sealing me inside and killing the outside light. *We just might need those hostages after all.*

FIFTEEN

The Union ship emerged from the rift right as *The Renegade Star* was leaving the planet's thermosphere.

As we did, the clarity of our long-range sensors improved and I was able to find the exact designation of the incoming vessel.

It was the *UFS Galactic Dawn*.

"Fuck," I said as I watched the rift close behind the oversized death ship.

"What do we do?" asked Abigail. She'd followed me into the cockpit, refusing to stay in the lounge. I saw no point in arguing this time.

Our thrusters eased when we were clear of the planet's gravity, and I aimed the ship toward a nearby moon. "We wait," I finally answered, trying to kill our momentum and bring us to a dead still. "As long as the cloak stays up, we should be good. We just can't move too much. A ship that size is bound to be able to see us. We need to keep our distance."

"Is that the only tunnel out of this system?"

"As far as I know," I said.

"That is affirmative, Abigail Pryar," answered Sigmond,

confirming my statement.

"Just Abigail, Sigmond," she corrected.

"Yes, Abigail," he acknowledged.

"Save the small talk, both of you. We need to find a way out of this. Better yet, we need to see how these bastards are tracking us."

"Do you think our hostages have some sort of transmitters on them?" asked Abigail.

I turned my head to look at her. It was the first time that thought had ever entered my brain, and I felt like a total idiot for it. "Can you go and ask them?"

"Now?" she asked. "Aren't we in the middle of something?"

"Seems like the best time, don't you think? If they have a transmitter, we need to get rid of it before we make another jump."

"I shall supervise the pat-down," said Sigmond. "I already scanned the soldiers, but perhaps further analysis will prove beneficial."

"Don't you need to help Jace?" asked Abigail.

"I can perform both services simultaneously."

I nodded. "He's a multitasker."

"Fine, I'm going," she said, getting up. "Try not to get us killed, Captain, if you don't mind."

I waited for her to leave. "No promises," I muttered, staring at the massive Union carrier on my holo display.

* * *

The Galactic Dawn had arrived out of the slip tunnel and gone nowhere. If I hadn't known any better, I might have thought it was abandoned.

If only I could be so lucky, I thought, trying to imagine a scenario, during slipspace travel, where the entire crew of thirty-thousand could have evacuated the ship. Too bad that would never happen, given the dangers involved. For example, veering off course in the middle of a tunnel could result in a ship hitting the surrounding walls, which nearly always resulted in disintegration of whatever matter it came into contact with.

No, there were people on that vessel. Tens of thousands, all following the orders of a man named General Marcus Brigham. He'd been tasked with hunting me and my crew down, all so the Union could dissect the little pale-faced girl sitting in my lounge.

Assholes, the lot of them, coming for a kid like her. I'd kill every last one, if I had to, before I let them touch her.

Special bonus if it meant saving my own ass in the process.

My eyes lingered on the holo image of the ship, wondering what the man in charge was thinking. Had he taken this assignment because he believed in the Union? Did he think kidnapping and dissecting a little girl was the righteous thing to do?

"Sir, we're receiving a transmission," said Sigmond, almost

like an answer to my thoughts.

"Let's hear it," I said, leaning forward with my arms on my knees.

The speaker clicked a few times, followed by a moment of silence, and then…

"This is General Marcus Brigham with the *UFS Galactic Dawn* hailing Captain Jace Hughes of *The Renegade Star*. Respond."

The sound of my own name gave me pause. It was strange hearing the old man speak it, almost unsettling.

"Again, this is General Brigham, speaking directly to Jace Hughes," continued the voice. "Captain, it is in your best interest to turn yourself in, along with the stolen cargo in your possession. I assure you, if you cooperate with me, I can ease your sentencing. You have an hour to respond to this request, after which I will have little choice but to use force. This doesn't have to be difficult, Captain Hughes."

I smirked. "Difficult, he says. That's a polite way of saying he doesn't want to chase or fight me, just for me to give up now and save him the trouble. Great deal."

"Sir," began Sigmond. "You may be interested to know that the signal from the *UFS Galactic Dawn* is being sent to a specific section of the system."

"What do you mean?" I asked.

"The transmission, sir. It is being sent directly to our present location."

"That can't be right. Are you sure they're not just sending it to one area at a time? They could be doing it to see when we respond, which would narrow down the search."

"No, sir," he answered. "The transmission is targeting our exact position. That is, within one hundred kilometers."

"Shit..." I felt my stomach turn. "The only way they can do that is if they know where we are, but the only way that's possible is if they can track us, but that would mean..."

And then it hit me, like a bag of shit from the sky. I suddenly knew why, no matter how far we moved, no matter how many tunnels we took, the Union always stayed a step behind us, never slowing down. It all made so much sense that I couldn't believe I hadn't thought of it before.

"The cloak," I finally said. "This whole time, they've been using our fucking cloak!"

* * *

I had Sigmond remain on standby while I took off through the ship, passing Hitchens and Freddie in the lounge as I ran to the cargo bay. If anyone could tell me what I wanted to know, it would be the two guests we had stowed away in our makeshift cell.

"Open the wall!" I called as I entered the upper level of the bay.

Abigail was still here, rifle in hand. "I already shook them down, but they didn't have any transmitters."

"I'm not here for that," I said, climbing down the stairs. I ran over to the cell wall as it began to slide up.

"Then, what? Did you figure something else out?" she asked.

I pulled out my pistol. "Stand back."

Alphonse and Docker were inside, their backs against the wall. They cringed when the light from the carbo bay hit them, like a couple of otherworldly fiends. "Is there something we can do for you, Captain?" asked Alphonse, his hand over his eyes.

I raised my pistol and pointed it squarely at Docker's forehead. "You can tell me how the *fuck* Brigham is tracking my cloak!" I looked at Alphonse. "Untie this idiot."

He slowly moved closer to Docker and undid the knot around his mouth.

Docker shook his head, once he could talk. "I-I don't know anything."

"Liar," I said, feeling an itch in my trigger finger. "Tell me the truth or I'll start firing. You think I give two shits about keeping you alive, Docker? You tried to escape and hurt my crew. If you don't start giving me information, you're worthless to me."

Docker crouched, hiding behind his arms. "I really don't know! Don't shoot me, please!"

Alphonse stood there, watching the two of us. "They're here, aren't they?" he asked.

"What?" I said.

"The Union," he explained. "They finally showed up, didn't

they?"

I had to give him credit. He was quick to piece things together. Smarter than Docker, at least. "They have, and the only way any of us survive, yourselves included, is if I figure out how they found us."

"What makes you think we know?" he asked.

"Maybe you don't, but something tells me you don't want to die in this cell."

He slowly nodded. "All they want is the girl, right? Why not just turn her over? Isn't that the safer move?"

"Why would I ever consider doing that? You think I'm that heartless?"

He shrugged. "You're a Renegade, right? Isn't that part of your job description? You work for money, not people."

"Being a Renegade isn't just about money," I said.

"Oh? Then, what's it about?"

"Whatever you want it to be, and right now it's about staying alive and out of a Union prison cell, and protecting the people on this ship. So, one of you had better start telling me exactly how Brigham is tracking me. If it's really my cloak, then I want to know."

The ensign stared at me with a strange expression, like he was deciding something. Maybe it was whether or not I'd kill him if he didn't give me what I wanted to know. Maybe he just wondered if I'd really sacrifice my ship just to save a little kid.

"I'm just an ensign," he finally said. "I don't know everything, but I'll tell you what I can. You asked about the cloak and the answer is yes. That's what they're using to track you. If you stop using it, they won't have a beacon to follow anymore."

"I knew it," I said, looking back at Docker. "You lied to me, you scrawny little spitfuck."

"He didn't know about it," said Alphonse. "He was telling the truth."

"It's true!" said Docker.

"How can an ensign know more than you, Docker? That doesn't make any sense."

"I'm a command officer," said Alphonse. "The information is compartmentalized. He doesn't know because he doesn't have to."

I moved my gun over to Alphonse. "In that case, tell me what you know about the cloak, and make it quick."

"You bought that cloak off a black-market trader, right?"

"Sure," I said, picturing the recently deceased Fratley.

"And when you purchased it, where did the merchant say they found it?"

"Union territory, but I don't know the specifics," I said.

"Well, let me fill in the gaps," said Alphonse. "Modern cloaking technology was first developed in the Union's thirty-second research center, also known as T.R.U.S.T." He looked behind me at Abigail. "Your friend back there knows all about that place. It's where she stole the girl."

Abigail walked up beside me. "Watch yourself," she cautioned.

"Sorry," he said, sounding genuine. "As I was saying, T.R.U.S.T. developed cloaking technology, and since then, only Union vessels have been allowed to use it. The Sarkonians managed to get their hands on some parts a few decades ago, so they have a handful of ships outfitted with it, but those have all been modified with a custom frequency by the Sarkonian government. Most of them are also outdated, since those people don't really innovate so much as steal and modify."

"Get to the point," I said with my gun still on him.

"This ship, your *Renegade Star*, is outfitted with a fairly advanced cloak. That should tell you it didn't come from the Sarkonians."

"I already know it's from a Union ship," I said.

"Good," he responded. "So, knowing that, what conclusions can you draw?"

I didn't like this game, him leading me along, and me trying to piece together the clues. I couldn't deny his subtle pokes, however, as I was now beginning to understand. "You're saying that because my cloak came from the Union, they can track me."

"Very good, Captain!" he exclaimed, genuine excitement in his voice. "You've figured it out. Yes, the cloak in your possession was once part of a Union ship, as you said, which means it can be tracked. That's how General Brigham has been following you, ever since you started running."

"If that's true, why didn't the Union come after me before? I've been using this cloak for months."

He chuckled. "What use would there be in that? What would they have to gain?"

"It's stolen tech. Why wouldn't they want it back?"

"Captain, there are bigger things at play here than the theft and reacquisition of a single cloak. Had you never adopted the nun and child, I can assure you none of this would have happened."

"How do I make it so they can't track us?"

He shrugged. "I'm sorry, but I'm not an engineer. I really don't know except to suggest you keep from using it."

"That's too bad, because I'm not surrendering, which means the only way you survive any of this is if I get away. You'd better think of something if you want to make it out of here alive."

"As much as I value self-preservation, I'm afraid I really have no idea. Trust me, Captain, I don't have any loyalty to the Union. I just work for them."

Something told me that was only half-true. "Cut the shit and tell me who you are?"

"I already did. My name is Alphonse. You know that."

"I don't know anything," I said.

He gave me a thin smile. "You're certainly right about that, Captain."

SIXTEEN

"What's your plan?" asked Abigail, once we had sealed the prisoners away.

I walked swiftly to the stairs. There was little time to waste, now that I had confirmation about the cloak. I'd have to find a way around Brigham's ship without my ability to hide. It wasn't going to be an easy escape.

"I'm still working on that," I said, stopping at the cargo bay entrance. I paused to look at her, and she nearly ran into me. "What are you doing?"

"I'm coming with you, obviously."

"I don't have time to entertain you," I told her. "I need to get to the bridge and think about how—"

"We'll do it together," she said, interrupting me. "I'll help you figure it out, Jace."

The com in my ear clicked. "Sir, the *UFS Galactic Dawn* is on the move. What are your orders?"

Had it already been an hour? No, that couldn't be possible. I'd only been down here for twenty minutes at the most.

I touched my ear. "What do you mean, 'on the move'? On the

move to where?"

"Here, sir," answered Sigmond. "They're on a direct course to our location."

"Guess that confirms they can see us," I said.

"Then, we need to find a way to avoid them," said Abigail. "Without the cloak, of course."

"I don't know if that's possible," I answered.

We ran through the hall and back to the bridge, taking our seats in a hurry. As I buckled my harness, I heard someone yelling from the lounge. "What's going on?"

It sounded like Hitchens.

"Oh, my goodness. Are we under attack?"

Definitely Hitchens.

"How do we play this one, Jace?" asked Abigail.

The holo showed the Galactic Dawn as it moved in our direction. I only had a few seconds to think my way out of this, and I wouldn't have a cloak to back me up. I'd relied on it for so long, going without it felt like moving backwards.

"Jace?" repeated Abigail. She grabbed me by the shoulder. "Hey! Are you listening to me?"

I examined the layout of this system and the positions of the two ships—ours and Brigham's. There was enough space between us to allow for a good run, but it would all come down to the location of the slip tunnel. "Yeah, I hear you," I said to Abigail. "And I've got this shit."

With a swipe of my finger, I activated the ship's engines, pulling us away from the moon. I dropped the cloak right as we broke orbit and set our course towards the nearby planet.

"Siggy, where's the next slip tunnel, not including the one we took to get here?"

"Two million kilometers beyond the farthest planetoid in this system. Shall I chart a course?"

"How long would it take to get there?"

"Approximately ten minutes."

"Think we got a chance to make it out of this alive?"

"Roughly fifty-two percent, sir."

I took a breath. *I should learn to stop asking him that.*

The Galactic Dawn moved toward us, even as we made our way to the other side of the planet. I could sense Abigail's anxiety building. She was tough, I knew, but one of the flagships of the Union was bearing down on us. Even I felt sick to my stomach.

When the tension was at its thickest, Abigail finally asked, "I really hope you know what you're doing, Jace, otherwise we're all dead!"

"Just watch," I said, nodding towards the giant ball of plasma as we grew closer. "That star is our ticket out of here."

As *The Galactic Dawn* continued its pursuit, it came within close orbital distance around the gas giant. I made certain to stay on the exact opposite side at all times, rotating with it.

I pressed the controls forward, sending us to the planet at a

90-degree angle from where *The Galactic Dawn* was heading. If you were to look at the planet from the center, it would have appeared like we'd cut down the middle of it, coming up from below, while *The Galactic Dawn* continued its pursuit from left to right.

That was the great thing about space travel. Every direction was forward, depending on your perspective.

In this case, what appeared to be the bottom of the gas giant to General Brigham was simply another route to freedom for me.

This alone wouldn't save us, I knew, but it was a fine start.

"The *UFS Galactic Dawn* is deploying fighters," announced Sigmond. "I'm estimating over two hundred, heading in our direction."

As we broke free of the planet's gravity, I set our course toward the second tunnel. "Why are you going that far out?" asked Abigail when she saw what I was doing. "Why not use the way we came in from?"

"If Brigham followed us here, there's probably reinforcements waiting on the other side. We need to use another route if we don't want to die the second we come out of slipspace."

"How do you know he left reinforcements?" she asked.

"Because," I continued. "That's what I would do if I were him."

The Galactic Dawn's fighters appeared on the radar, lighting up like a plague of insects. I'd never seen so many in all my life, but I knew it wouldn't matter. All I had to do was beat them to the slip tunnel.

"Sir, Union fighters are approaching," informed Sigmond.

"I see them, pal," I said, spotting what appeared to be fifteen dots blinking their way to our location.

I searched the system for cover, but there wasn't much to use. The cloak clearly wasn't an option, which meant I'd have to play this the old-fashioned way.

I pointed *The Star* at the nearby asteroid cluster. "Time for a game of hide-and-find."

Abigail snapped a look at me. "Wait a second, we can't just go into that!"

I grinned. "Have a little faith, Abigail. You're a nun, after all."

"Former nun!" she yelled.

A dozen fighters were gaining on us as we arrived at the asteroid cluster. As we neared the first set of rocks, an alarm sounded on the dash. "Enemy ships are within firing distance, sir."

The cockpit shook rapidly as we took a blast in our ass. "In we go!" I shouted, gripping the controls with both my hands, bringing us between two moon-sized boulders.

The ships at our rear followed closely, moving quickly to keep up. The shield around *The Star* deflected some light debris as we dove beneath one of the rocks.

The others continued their pursuit, maintaining their speed.

I spotted a denser section of the field. "Hold on tight," I told Abigail. "Siggy, release the mines on my mark."

"Understood."

Three rocks were so close they nearly created a tunnel between them, so I took it, entering through the gap. "Now!" I barked.

Six small mines deployed from the base of our ship, activating three seconds afterwards, hovering in the empty space between the stones.

The strike ships followed, going into the gap. As they did, the mine activated, creating an explosion that disintegrated the first, but sent the next five into the rocks.

We escaped the narrow opening a second later, flying back into the open asteroid field. "Six ships down," informed Siggy.

The remaining ships continued their pursuit, firing and blasting *The Star's* rear shield. I felt the burst when it landed, shaking the entire cockpit and sending the little Foxy Stardust bobblehead into the air. "Hot fucking hell!" I snapped.

"What is it?!" asked Abigail, no doubt sensing my panic. "Do they have us?"

"My Foxy bobble almost bit the dust," I growled, reaching for the toy and planting it back on my dash. "There. We're good now."

"Goddammit, Jace!" snapped the former nun.

Another shot hit us and a red warning light came on, informing me that if I didn't lose these guys soon, I'd be in some serious shit.

I steered *The Star* toward one of the larger asteroids, cutting so close to the rock that it penetrated my shield and set off a proximity alarm.

The other ships followed, trying to keep up. "Get ready to take the flight controls, Siggy," I said as we came around the asteroid at a perpendicular angle.

"I shall set a direct course for the slip tunnel," he responded.

Three ships were hot on our tail. "Okay, then," I muttered, spotting a large cluster of rocks ahead of us.   I squeezed the control stick and glanced at Abigail. "Hold on to your trousers!"

Abigail's eyes widened as she saw what was coming. "What the—"

I pulled the stick back, spinning the ship to angle us perfectly between the initial wall of floating stones. As soon as we were through the first layer, I took the ship straight up with a hard turn, taking the cleanest path out of the field.

The other ships tried to stay close and avoid the asteroids, but all it took was a single mistake, made by the first pilot as he nicked one of the rocks with his wing. The collision destabilized his flightpath and sent him spiraling out of control, creating a chain effect with the other ships, knocking each of them off course. Only one managed to pull through, despite some slight damage to its forward compartment.

I checked the scanner to find a shitload of dots still after us, but they were far enough behind that they'd never reach us. Only the one remaining fighter was close enough to warrant concern.

Now that we were clear of the asteroids, I'd have no choice but to take him out myself.

"Are we nearly there?" asked Abigail, gripping the seat handles.

I gave her a wink, then cut the engines, turning us around in a complete 180. We continued flying, only now we were backwards, facing the enemy ship as it quickly closed the gap on us.

With my thumbs on the quad-cannon triggers, I watched the Union strike ship come within firing distance.

"Warning," announced Sigmond. "Enemy vessel is closing."

The ship fired a quick spread on us, mostly missing, but still managing to graze the hull. I felt my seat tremble. *Almost there,* I thought as I waited, hoping to make this count.

Finally, the holo gave me the green, lining up the best possible shot, and I squeezed the trigger.

The blast struck the strike ship directly in the cabin, tearing through its hull like a knife through paper, and it exploded from the inside out.

"There it is!" I barked, feeling the adrenaline as it coursed through my veins.

An indicator light blinked, letting me know that another wave was fast approaching. "If you're finished having fun," said Abigail, motioning to the radar.

"Right," I said, then turned the ship and lit the engines. "Siggy, start the slipspace sequence and get that tunnel open!"

"Already processing," said the A.I. "Opening slip tunnel in five seconds."

"Captain Jace Hughes," said a deep voice over the com. "This is General Brigham. I know you're receiving this message. I implore you to respond."

I clenched my teeth. "Siggy, open the channel."

"Ready when you are, sir."

"Brigham, this is Captain Hughes of *The Renegade Star*. You'd best turn your ass around and head home, because you'll never get what you're after."

There was a short pause. "Captain Hughes, I see you've finally decided to talk back," said the General.

"I've done more than talked, haven't I?"

"That you have, Captain. It seems the reports I've read about you are true."

"Glad I was able to satisfy. It's probably been a while since you had a good fuck," I said.

He laughed, but it sounded more forced than genuine. "Hughes, why don't you cut your engines and hand over the girl? You have my word that I'll let you go."

"That's a generous offer," I said, glancing at Abigail, who was waiting beside me with a tense expression. "What about the rest of my crew?"

"They can go as well, sir. Your entire crew, even the woman

who stole her, can walk away from this. All we want is the girl. The rest is negotiable."

I paused, staring at the holo of the Galactic Dawn. It was so big, so majestic, like a god compared to me and mine. I was nothing to this man, just a piece of shit who had what he wanted. Any other day, he would have walked over my corpse and never thought a thing about it. Not that I could blame him.

"There's an issue I take with that, if you don't mind me saying, General."

"Whatever it is, I'm sure we can—"

"The little girl you want, the one with the tattoos and the stupid questions…she's as much a part of this crew as me, and I ain't letting her go. Not with the Union. Not with the Sarkonians—" A crack in space opened and a green swirling light appeared before us. "—and especially not with you."

I clicked the com off. "The slipspace tunnel is open. Please proceed forward," said Sigmond.

I eased the ship into the tunnel, disappearing inside.

"Wait a second," said Abigail. "Where does this passage come out at?"

Sigmond's answer came immediately. "According to the star chart, the next slip gap point along this path is…" The holo transformed into a map of the star cluster, zooming in on the destination in question. "The center of Sarkonian space, approximately six million kilometers from Sarkon, their capital planet."

Abigail and I looked at one another right as we entered the rift. "Shit," we each said, turning back to the green light as it continued to surround our ship.

SEVENTEEN

"Dammit, Siggy!" I barked, slamming my fist on the console in front of me. "Why didn't you tell me where this thing went before we got inside?"

"Apologies, sir, but you didn't ask," responded Sigmond.

I went to yell at him a second time, but stopped, choosing instead to count to ten. "One. Two. Three."

"What are you doing?" asked Abigail.

"Trying my best not to shoot my own ship, if I'm being honest."

"Well, don't. I need you to keep your head on straight if we're going to make it out of this."

"I won't murder Siggy today, but not because you told me not to."

Heading deeper into Sarkonian space, especially their homeworld, was not something I was eager to do. Not only was it dangerous for someone with fake papers like me, but we'd already encountered their military, and somehow they'd known all about the bounties on our heads, despite the fact that the Union and the Sarkonian Empire never worked together on anything before. For them to discard decades of rivalry, distrust, and animosity just to turn in a few bounties seemed more than unrealistic. It was just plain ridiculous.

No, there had to be more to it than that. Something bigger that I couldn't see. I had to figure this shit out.

"Where are you going?" Abigail asked as I was getting to my feet.

"To interrogate our prisoners about what to expect when we arrive," I explained. "We know the Union and the Sarkonians are working together, but we need to find out why. Since we can't access the gal-net inside slipspace, those two jackasses are our only leads."

"I'll come with you."

"No, stay here and help Siggy monitor the tunnel," I ordered, opening the door. I stepped out into the lounge.

"Isn't that something he does on his own?" she asked, right as the door slid shut.

"It sure is," I said in a low voice as I continued through the ship.

I'd never been in the heart of Sarkonian space. Like the Union, it was a region I generally ignored, if I could help it.

I'd only encountered the Sarkonians a handful of times, although those instances had spiked in recent weeks, thanks to the blunder back in Spiketown.

I entered the cargo bay and took the stairs. "Open the wall,

Siggy," I said, unholstering my pistol.

The door slid up, revealing the two prisoners. Alphonse sat with his legs crossed on the floor, while Docker remained in the far corner, sitting much further away, arms tied and the gag back around his mouth. The light from the bay hit them both, but only Docker flinched.

"Back already?" asked Alphonse.

"Take your friend's gag off," I ordered, motioning at Docker with my gun.

"Yes, Captain," said the young man, politely. He unwrapped the cloth from Docker's mouth, but it was tightly bound, making it difficult to remove. After some yanking, which I could tell was unpleasant, based on Docker's expression, Alphonse managed to get it free, discarding the gag on the floor.

Docker stretched his jaw and licked his chapped lips, squinting at me as he drew close enough for more outer light to touch him. He let out an exasperated groan. "Thank you for finally—"

"Shut up," I demanded. "Tell me why the Sarkonians know about the bounties on me and my crew. They're on a separate network. They don't use the gal-net. Why would they bother looking us up and turning us in?"

He wrinkled his nose. "I don't know a lot about that."

"Sure, you do," I countered. "I bet you both know plenty."

"The only thing I've seen is the Sarkonians are working with the Union to find this ship, but that's all," he insisted.

"You don't know why they agreed to it?"

He shook his head. "Wish I did. Really!"

"Is that really all you know, Docker?" I cocked the hammer on the pistol, and it echoed through the bay. "Are you sure there's not something you're leaving out?"

"I-I told you the truth a second ago, I swear! There's nothing else really at all, I swear to all the gods!" he was talking so fast I thought he might pass out. The crippling anxiety in his voice told me everything I needed to know.

"Fine." I couldn't tell if there was any other information in that idiot worth pulling out. For now, I'd have to assume he'd given me everything and rely on Alphonse for the rest. I turned and pointed the gun at him. "Your turn, kid."

He eyed the barrel. "I see."

"Start talking. This gun is getting heavy, and I'd sooner shoot you both than keep it raised."

"You might not like what I have to say, Captain. How do I know you won't shoot me just because you're angry?"

"I need you to keep my people alive. If you help me do that, I won't hurt you," I said. "But, if I find out you're bullshitting me, I'll kill every last piece of you."

He stared at me for a few seconds, a cold, emotionless look on his face. I couldn't tell if he was planning a surprise attack, plotting an escape, or recounting his favorite soap opera, his face was so empty. "All right, Captain Hughes. I'll tell you what you want to know."

This fucking guy, I thought, staring into those strange eyes.

He cleared his throat. "Docker is correct. The Sarkonians are working with the Union, but what he didn't say is that they aren't in this for the bounty on your head."

"How's that, now?" I asked.

"The Union offered the Sarkonian government a truce, allowing them direct access to 50% of Deadland space without having to worry about Union interference."

I considered this for a moment, laying out the star map in my head. The Deadlands made up a large chunk of space, with dozens of systems in it, all of it between the borders of the Union and Sarkonian Empire. Most of the region was utterly lawless, which made it easy for folk like me to come and go. The Union and the Sarkonians remained content to leave the uncivilized region to itself for the better part of two centuries. Until recently, of course, as I'd witnessed firsthand. "You mean the Union and the Sarkonians are planning to take over the Deadlands?"

"I don't know if the Union means to conquer their side of the Deadlands adjacent to their border. The dominant view right now in Ambrosia is that it's too much work to police it all. There's also not enough resources there to make the expansion worthwhile." He crossed his arms. "But the Sarkonians are different. They're restricted to half a dozen sectors and a handful of systems within their own territory. They have no other choice but to expand, which means they need the Deadlands, even if the worlds are remote, chaotic, and disorganized."

"Wait a second here," I said, waving my pistol. "Are you saying the Union's going to let them expand their borders just for capturing us?"

He grinned. "That's exactly what I'm telling you, Captain."

"But that's crazy. The Sarkonians are violent and stupid. The Union hates them. Why would they make a deal like that?"

With his arms still crossed, Alphonse opened his palm and leaned forward, like he was inviting me to connect the dots. "What do you have that they want?"

"Wait, you're saying it's because of Lex?"

He nodded. "The one and only."

"But, why go through all that trouble for just one kid?"

"Ah, now that's the real question, isn't it?" asked Alphonse with a slight smirk. "Why risk your very security, all to procure a single child? I must admit, Captain, I'm also in the dark, but I'm oh-so fascinated to learn the truth."

I scoffed at the idea of it all. The Union was willing to risk their own security, their own borders, just to find my ship and the little albino.

"You know too much to be some shitty ensign," I said, looking at his rank insignia. A single yellow bar on his collar.

"Do I?" he asked, not hiding his amusement. "I suppose that's true."

I took a step back and lowered the gun. Tapping my ear, I said, "Drop the door. I'm done here."

"Yes, sir," said Sigmond, and the wall began to slide down.

"Until next time, Captain Hughes," called Alphonse. "Please, do try not to die."

* * *

I gathered everyone in the lounge. Freddie, Abigail, Hitchens, and Octavia. Meanwhile, Siggy managed to distract Lex with a game in her room. She didn't need to hear any of this.

"Please tell me you have a plan," said Abigail.

"Did the prisoners give you any information?" asked Octavia.

I nodded. "It's not good news, in case you're wondering."

"Of course it's not," said Abigail. "Why should we expect otherwise?"

"Basically," I continued, ignoring the nun's sass. "The Union made a deal with the Sarkonians for our heads. If they deliver us to Brigham, they get to invade the Deadlands, uncontested."

Hitchens dropped his jaw. "A-Are you being serious?"

"That does seem like a stretch, just to capture us," said Freddie, who looked equally surprised.

Abigail pressed her fingers to the bridge of her nose, closing her eyes. "Gods."

"I didn't believe it at first, either," I said.

"Are you certain the intelligence on this is good?" asked Freddie.

"No, I'm not, but Alphonse was right about the cloak, so maybe he's telling the truth."

"I can't believe they'd go this far just to stop us and capture Lex." Freddie shook his head. "All this for a little girl who never did anything wrong."

I glanced down at Octavia, who was sitting quietly in her wheelchair. She seemed to be lost in thought, her eyes drifting along the floor to the base of the wall. "You have anything to add, Octavia?"

She blinked, looking at me. "Hm? Oh, I apologize, Captain. I was thinking..."

"How's that going for you?" I asked.

She stroked her wrist with her index finger for several seconds, like she was trying to put her thoughts together. "I believe the ensign was telling you the truth."

"You do?" I asked. "You got a hunch about it?"

"It's far more than that," she explained. "Do you recall the information I shared with you about Lex's biology?"

"Sure," I said, looking at Abigail. "Something about fast healing and perfect cell replication."

"Close enough. I've been busy working on it."

Abigail stiffened. "Have you found anything more?"

"We already know the cells in her body are perfect. They

perform tasks with optimal efficiency, without deterioration, hence the lack of scarring as well as her incredible healing. However, such a thing is impossible in nature, at least as we know it. I wasn't sure at first, but it must be artificial. I don't know how, but someone found a way to create a genetically perfect human being."

She paused, perhaps expecting someone to speak, but we were all caught up in what she was saying that none of us felt the need. All our eyes were on Octavia. "I've found no trace of any modification, even after testing her several times and repeatedly biopsying her cells. Thanks to the equipment we procured from the medical station, I can finally tell you that there is no sign of post-natal engineering. By that I mean, I do not believe the Union ever changed her DNA sequencing or cell behavior once she was out of the womb. I think she was born this way."

"But you just said the changes weren't natural," said Freddie.

"Correct," she confirmed. "I believe this was done *to* her, either in the womb or as a simple embryo. I have no way of knowing, not without an entire lab and staff at my disposal, but it's currently my working theory, given the technology at our disposal. I could be completely wrong and maybe the Union really did do this to her, but considering the reports about how she was found, it stands to reason that she origins are elsewhere, someplace beyond Union control. They found her on a fringe planet in an insignificant village. She arrived there in a small pod of unknown design. That's the story we've heard. It's what the report stated. We have no way to clarify it, even if we wanted to, but if it is all true, then somewhere in the galaxy, by some unknown organization or individual, Lex's true parentage is waiting. Who knows where they are or why they did it? But I firmly believe the ones responsible have yet to be found."

"All of this is sounding pretty outrageous," I said. "You're saying that Lex was made in a lab, but you don't know for sure, and you don't know when or why or by who. Is that about right?"

She nodded. "It's difficult for me to know, as I said, and I'm not an expert on human biology. I have six years of medical school, but there were people with a lifetime of experience in those Union facilities, working tirelessly with the best equipment available, and I suspect they didn't fully understand it, either."

"But that's why they want her back," said Abigail. "They know she's special. It's not just the tattoos and the way she affects the ancient Earth artifacts. It's her entire biology they're after."

"She's unique," agreed Octavia. "And that's what makes her dangerous."

I scoffed. "Dangerous? She's just a kid."

"Imagine an army, an entire military, with healing capabilities,' she cautioned. "Imagine the implications if the Union could weaponize that kind of genetic engineering."

"I'd rather not imagine it at all," said Freddie.

"Worse yet," said Hitchens. "The artifacts I've collected can only be powered by the child's markings. If Earth does indeed possess a more sophisticated collection, we might be looking at a potentially devastating new arsenal of weapons, the likes of which this galaxy has not seen in millennia." He tapped his chin. "As advanced as ancient Earth was said to be, its weaponry could be beyond our understanding."

Octavia lowered her eyes. "The strongest military power in the galaxy could become the *only* military power. Their conquest would be catastrophic."

"If all of that is true," muttered Freddie. "Then, it's no wonder they're willing to let the Sarkonians encroach on the Deadlands. If they have Lex and Earth, then what do a few more systems matter?"

"If nothing else," continued Octavia. "This confirms what we have suspected. The Union will do anything to repossess what we stole, no matter the cost."

I knew what I was hearing was out there, but it also made a certain kind of sense. The Union had sent their most powerful ship after us, with a seasoned General at the helm, and hundreds of strike ships. They'd made a deal with the Sarkonians, of all groups, just for the chance at getting Lex again. There was no other reason to do those things and take so many risks except if the ends justified the means. It was the most insane shit I'd ever heard in my life, but it was real and it was happening…and I was locked squarely in the center of it.

"Doesn't matter," I said, hooking my thumb on my belt. "That kid ain't going anywhere, 'cept with us."

Octavia nodded. "A statement we can all agree upon."

"Captain, if I might be so bold," said Hitchens, clearing his throat. "What is your plan, moving forward? Do you have one yet?"

I glanced out the window, staring at the green glow of the slipspace tunnel. "I'll let you know as soon as I do, Doc. For now, let's just worry about staying ahead of all the people trying to kill us."

He swallowed. "Dear me."

EIGHTEEN

Siggy scanned the system the second the tunnel opened. Before it was closed, he had a read-out of everything from the number of planetoids to a light scan of the Sarkonian homeworld, Sarkon. More importantly, he had a tally of every ship in the system, most of them militarized.

"This doesn't look good," Abigail said as the information started coming in over the holo.

I couldn't disagree. I had expected there to be dozens, perhaps even hundreds, of Sarkonian ships flying in and around Sarkon, but I never believed we'd see the fleet, itself, sitting at the other end of this tunnel. I'd assumed they'd be off near the border, assaulting Badland colonies or clashing with neighboring raiders, not waiting here by their lonesome... all for us.

No, not waiting. They couldn't have known *The Star* would show up, unless the Union had told them.

But, if that had been the case, wouldn't they have met us head-on, the second we entered the system? They had to be here for some other reason, right?

I pushed the question out of my head. There were more

pressing concerns right now than what the Sarkonian fleet was up to. For starters, we had the Union after us, and it wouldn't take them long to get here. Brigham would arrive in minutes, bringing hundreds of strike ships with him, all with the sole purpose of capturing us.

No, wait. That wasn't right, I had to remind myself. The old bastard wasn't after me. I was nothing to the Union but a Renegade with a deathwish. They only wanted the kid, and they'd do whatever it took to get her back, because she was a prize. A weapon to be used.

But only if I let them.

"Siggy, how many tunnels branch off from this system?" I asked, trying to focus.

"Sarkon lies at the center of a large intersection of slip tunnels. There are eight connecting paths, making this one of the most prominent slip gap points in the region," explained the A.I.

"That's a lot of options," muttered Abigail. "Which one of them takes us to where we want to go?"

"If you are referring to the course we previously charted, the corresponding tunnel lies on the other side of Sarkon, beyond the fleet. I am displaying coordinates now."

The holo changed, showing the entire system and all five planets, their moons, and anything large enough to qualify as a ship. Another dot blinked beyond Sarkon, near the fourth planet, indicating our new destination.

"Of course, we'd have to get around that fleet," I said, sighing. "Why can't you ever make it easy for me, Siggy?"

"Apologies, sir. I shall endeavor to do so in the future."

"How do you expect us to get around that?" asked Abigail.

I thought for a second, weighing the options. I could run for it, risk everything, hope for the best, maybe make it through somehow. Running and gunning had worked for me in the past. Hell, I just dodged the Galactic Dawn by doing just that, but the ships here were spread out too far, all across the system. It would be nearly impossible to get there without a fight. On the other hand, I could go around, leave the system, come back on the other side, but in doing so, I'd risk drawing attention through Sarkon's long-range detection grid. In fact, I was pretty sure they'd spot me soon if I didn't figure something out.

"We have to use the cloak," I finally said. "Siggy, you got that?"

"Right away, sir."

Abigail gave me a surprised look. "Didn't you say the Union was using your cloak to track us?"

"They're already on their way here, which means it doesn't matter."

"Why?" she asked.

"They already know where we went, and it's impossible to track us from inside the tunnel, which means they'll have to wait until they come out again. That gives us a few minutes where we can use the cloak safely, without worrying about detection, get through this fleet, and grab a one-way ticket out of this shitstorm."

"I see," she said, working through the plan. "All we have to do is get to the tunnel before General Brigham arrives."

"Exactly," I said, motioning at the blinking dot on the holo. "We'll just have to hurry."

I plugged in the flight commands, bringing the ship away from the slip tunnel entrance and moving us towards our destination.

"Wait a second," said Abigail. "What if the Union showed the Sarkonians how to track your cloak?"

The question took me by surprise. "They wouldn't do that," I muttered. "It would give the Sarkonians too much power. They could use that to track Union ships. Think about it."

"That makes sense," she said.

"We'll be fine. Don't worry." I tried to sound convincing, but the truth was that I had no fucking idea what the Union would do. If everything Alphonse had told me was true, then they might actually be willing to give up classified information, so long as it meant finding my ship. Whatever the cost, just to get their key to Earth.

I swallowed, blinking a few times as we drew closer to the fleet. The holo changed, showcasing several of the Sarkonian ships, each with their emblems on the hull. Most of them had one or two quad cannons. The larger vessels carried more than that. Getting caught right now would mean the end of everything. The end of all of us.

As *The Renegade Star* flew closer to the planet, Sarkon, one of the orbital ships began to move. It curved toward us, heading in the direction of the tunnel we had just left. I pulled the ship to the left, moving out of the way, but it also brought us closer to one of the Sarkonian freighters, a bulking transport vessel at least seventy-five times the size of my own. I eased us back, slowing our momentum, letting the departing ship get past us before bringing *The Star* back on its previous path.

I breathed when we were on our way again, getting farther from the fleet.

Still nothing, I thought as I continued to monitor the other ships' movements. None of them appeared to notice us as we edged our way through the system. I had to keep thrusters at a minimum, which doubled our crawl-time. It was a necessary sacrifice, as a large burst of heat could reveal our position. Even with a cloak, I still had to mind my actions.

It took about ten minutes to reach the tunnel's entrance. Only a few ships were lingering nearby, likely having just arrived. One or two seemed to be prepping to depart, which was good news for us. Each of the vessels took off toward Sarkon, one-at-a-time, leaving us alone after only a few minutes.

I was about to give the order to open the tunnel when Siggy's voice chimed in. "Sir, a slipspace tunnel is opening on the far side of the system. I believe it is the *UFS Galactic Dawn.*"

I glanced down at the holo display to see that he was indeed correct. The Union starship was arriving. "Siggy, drop our cloak," I ordered.

"Understood," said the A.I.

Abigail tensed, leaning forward as she watched *The Galactic Dawn* emerge from the rift. She looked like she was about to say something when Siggy interjected.

"Picking up a transmission," he said. "Sarkon is contacting the *UFS Galactic Dawn.*"

"Can we listen in?" I asked.

"Affirmative. Patching through now."

There was a short pause, followed by a few seconds of static, and then...

"...ome in, Union vessel! Halt your trajectory and stand down at once! You are in violation of sanction three-two-six-nine of the Androsia Convention! Stand down at once!"

A familiar voice answered almost immediately. "Sarkonian fleet, this is General Marcus Brigham. I am in pursuit of a fugitive ship passing through your system. The Union and Sarkonian Empire have agreed to work together to retrieve the runaway ship, so I suggest you suspend your aggression."

This time, a woman's voice answered. "General Brigham, this is High Commander Prynn Deschalla of the Sarkonian Empire. You have not been authorized to enter this system. I strongly advise you to return to your previous destination."

"Perhaps I was unclear," said the General. "I am pursuing a

fugitive ship known as *The Renegade Star*. We already have an agreement with you—"

"That agreement only permits your ship to enter specific systems within the Sarkonian Empire's territory. That does not include Sarkon. Your being here is inexcusable."

"With all due respect, if you would simply let me continue my mission, I—"

"We must insist that you return, General! This is not up for debate or negotiation. If there is a fugitive in our system, we shall recover them, not you. That was the agreement we signed, if you'll remember."

"There's no time for an argument," said Brigham. "Either step aside or help me, but decide quickly. I don't have all day to sit here and—"

A single Sarkonian ship, which the holo designated as *The Panchello*, fired a missile towards the bow of *The Galactic Dawn*, hitting its shield.

The com went dead, cutting off the moment the blast struck.

"Here we go," I muttered.

Suddenly, a mass firefight ensued, with *The Galactic* Dawn returning shots toward the mounting fleet, striking several at once and disabling them.

The Sarkonian fleet retaliated together, bombarding the Union carrier with hundreds of missiles, each one colliding with the massive shield. It wouldn't be long before they managed to penetrate The Galactic Dawn's defenses, though they were sure to suffer heavy losses.

Strike ships exited from the ship, setting their sights on the Sarkonians in quick time. The two fleets engaged, creating an impromptu warzone.

"Now, Siggy!" I barked. "Open the tunnel while they're killing each other."

"Doing so now," said the A.I.

A glowing rift formed ahead of us, splitting the darkness. I held the controls and pushed us forward, easing us into the center.

I was about to let myself relax when the cockpit jerked sideways and a warning light came on; we'd just been struck by a missile. The force of the inertial shift forced Abigail from her seat, slamming her into the console. I caught her arm before she could fall on the floor.

"Captain Hughes, stand down," said a female's voice over the com. It sounded vaguely familiar. "This is Commander Mercer Equestri. Surrender now or we *will* fire a second time."

"Siggy, raise shields!" I snapped.

Our shields went up fast, just in time to take the following attack from the incoming vessel. Before I could say anything else, a woman's face appeared on my holo. She had a scar across her face, and I recognized her immediately. "Stop where you are, Captain Hughes!"

"Shit, I didn't think I'd ever see that woman again," I muttered.

"What is she doing here?" asked Abigail, still in my arms.

I eased her back onto her seat. "If I only knew," I said, shaking my head. "I thought we were clear of her."

"Captain," continued Mercer, who could neither see nor hear me. "If you think I'm letting you through this tunnel, you're—"

I grabbed the controls. "Siggy, take us into the tunnel as fast as you can! Disregard safety protocols! Move!"

"As you wish, sir."

I tabbed the console, unloading one of my mines behind us, and raising the shield once the bomb was clear. With the mine at our rear, I pressed the activation switch.

The explosion hit our shield, setting off several alarms throughout the ship, and sent us barreling forward, into the rift. We began to spin as we entered.

"Enemy vessel is charging weapons," said Sigmond.

"Doesn't matter!" I snapped, holding onto the control sticks, trying to level us out. We continued to turn as we fell into the green tunnel. "We're in!"

The slipspace rift closed as we continued forward. *The Star* wavered, unsteadily, veering close to the tunnel wall. "Careful!" yelled Abigail.

"I know!" I shouted back, my hands all over the controls. Before I could actually level us, I felt the impact of the outer limits of the tunnel as we grazed the electrical field. I heard wrenching, tearing sounds coming from the hull, violently shaking the entirety of my ship. "Fuck!" I shouted, bracing myself for what I was sure to be a terrible rest of the day. "Hold on!"

NINETEEN

"Hull breach detected. Applying seals to surrounding units." Siggy's voice sounded like a distant whisper as *The Renegade Star* continued to spin out of control inside the slipspace tunnel.

"Do something, Jace!" yelled Abigail, gripping her seat to keep herself from getting thrown again.

I pulled back on the controls and hit the stabilizers, slowing our spin. "Siggy, try to compensate for—"

Before I could finish, I saw a tear form in front of us, signaling the end of this tunnel. "Exiting slip tunnel," announced Sigmond.

I pressed my hands on the console. "Already?!"

The tunnel light quickly faded as we left the opening and re-entered normal space. It closed quickly behind us and, much to my relief, everything went quiet and still. The chaos of the tunnel was suddenly gone.

"Siggy, what just happened? Did we make it?"

"You are correct, sir. According to the star chart that Doctor Hitchens provided, we have arrived at the next slip gap point."

I breathed a sigh of relief, but knew I couldn't slow down. "Chart a course for the next one, and hurry. We need to move as fast as we can. I'm sure I pissed off that Mercer gal somethin' bad."

"Sir, a quick note before we continue," said Sigmond.

"Go ahead, but make it quick," I said.

"This S.G. Point contains, multiple additional tunnels. Four, to be precise."

"Another intersection?" I asked. It was a surprise, considering how rare they were. No one knew exactly how tunnels formed or why so many ended and began near one another, but it was uncommon to find more than a few in one place. For us to encounter two different slip gap points, each with several tunnels, within the same few hours was highly unlikely.

"According to the atlas, our path is here," said Sigmond, and a map formed on the holo, highlighting our next destination, the third tunnel from our location.

"Let's keep going. We don't have time to waste sitting here," I said.

"Maybe we'll get lucky and our pursuers will think we took another path," said Abigail.

"We should expect the worst, although I like the optimism." Without taking any time to recover from any of the damage we took in the last one, I had Siggy open another tunnel. We were on the run now, for better or worse. "How long before we get there?" I asked.

"Fourteen lightyears to the next S.G. Point, then we have two other connections," said Sigmond. "Altogether, it will take us five hours to reach the end."

"Not bad," I said, taking the controls and maneuvering us into position. I was about to enter the tunnel when I stopped to consider an alternative. "Wait a second."

"Something wrong?" asked Abigail.

"Siggy, how many mines do we have left?" I asked.

"Six," he said.

"Not as much as I'd like, but it should do."

"What are you rambling about?" asked Abigail.

"The mines, obviously," I said.

It took her a second to realize what I was planning. "Wait a minute, Jace, you can't just drop those in the middle of nowhere at an S.G. Point. What if a civilian ship hits them?"

"We don't have time for an argument. What do you think is more likely, anyway? A bunch of schoolkids comes out this way...or we're followed by an army of pissed of Sarkonians? Did you see what I did to that Mercer woman's ship? She's coming after us with everything she's got."

"There's still a chance you might not hit her, though," said Abigail. "Think about the risks."

"I'll do what's necessary to keep this crew alive." I tabbed the console and began releasing several mines into the area, ordering them to disperse equally around the slip gap point. "If that means planting a few bombs in the middle of nowhere and not knowing who they'll end up hitting, then so be it. It's the best option on the table."

The look on Abigail's face told me she disapproved. Still, she didn't argue, and that meant she understood.

A rift formed and we entered it, passing into the new tunnel and leaving the S.G. Point behind. Whatever soul was unfortunate enough to follow us, I hoped they deserved what they found.

* * *

The lounge was half-destroyed when I got there, all the chairs and stools turned on their side. The contents of the fridge were all over the floor, too, as well as the Union coffeemaker I'd acquired from that ship.

Piece of shit, I thought as I glared at it before continuing to the side corridor.

Lex was sitting on her bed, swinging her legs back and forth with a curious expression. She watched as Freddie and Hitchens tried to pick up the room, since it was littered with tossed clothes. "Everyone okay?" I asked, leaning on the door frame.

Hitchens, with a pile of Octavia's shirts in his arms, waddled over to me. "Ah, Captain! I take it we've arrived safely? How fares the ship?"

"We're a little beat up, but we'll fly."

Freddie waved at me before tossing a small pile on Lex's head. She giggled and kicked a pair of pants at his face, smacking him in the forehead. "Hey!" he said, laughing. "You're playing dirty!"

"Well, looks like you're all fine," I said, trying not to look amused. "Where's Octavia?"

"She's in the cargo bay, checking on our lab equipment. I believe there was some damage to the microscope and blood samples, but nothing we can't replace," explained Hitchens.

"I need to see about our Union guests, anyway," I said.

"I wanna see her, too!" said Lex, jumping up from the bed and racing out of the room. She passed by me and I quickly jerked out of the way.

"Hey, slow down!" I called, but she was already gone.

"She's just excited," said Freddie.

"Better that than scared, I guess."

He nodded. "How are we looking with the map? Are we close yet?"

"We're a few hours from wherever it is we're going."

They both looked at one another. "Are you saying we're nearing Earth?" asked Freddie.

"No, I'm saying the map is almost done," I corrected. "Who the hell knows what we'll find?"

"Whatever it is," said Hitchens, "I only hope it leads us to the truth."

I left the two of them behind and made my way to the cargo bay. We didn't have much time before we arrived out of this tunnel, which meant whatever repairs we had to make would have to be done quickly.

Octavia was halfway through the hall when I found her, well on her way to the cargo bay. She had to move slowly, due to all the fallen junk in the middle of the floor. "You need some help?" I asked when I reached her.

"No, I believe I nearly have it," she wheezed, stretching to reach a piece of metal that had broken free of the wall and kept her from progressing. She swooped it up after a moment and set it to the side, against the wall.

"Looks like we took a beating, but so far nothing's seriously damaged," I said.

"We'll see. I haven't seen the lab equipment yet."

"I need to check on the prisoners, too," I said, taking the back of her wheelchair and pushing. "Let's see if we can speed this up."

"You're a gentleman," she remarked. "Just don't expect anything from me. I'm married to my work."

"What about Hitchens?" I asked with a light smirk.

"You should worry about your ship right now, Captain."

When we entered the upper deck of the cargo bay, I glanced around, looking for Lex. "Where's the kid?"

"She sped past me on the way. Maybe she's down the stairs?"

"Someone needs to strap her in so she doesn't keep running off," I suggested.

"She has too much energy for such a small space, that's all." Octavia rolled over to the table with the microscope. Several vials had fallen to the floor, shattered and broken. She didn't seem surprised or bothered by it.

I left her to handle her own business and ascended the stairs. I quickly noticed some damage to the retracting deck on the far side of the room. "Siggy, why didn't you report that?" I asked.

"Report what, sir?" responded the A.I.

"The fucked-up deck. Are your sensors okay?"

"Apologies, sir. It seems some of my damage detection is malfunctioning for this portion of the ship. I will need to analyze my sensors to initiate repairs."

"Great, so we need to fix something just so we can see what else needs to be fixed. Maybe we'll get lucky out here and run into a repair station."

"Highly unlikely," responded Sigmond, not quite getting my sarcasm.

I ignored him, walking out into the middle of the bay, scanning for the kid. "Lex, where are—"

I stopped when I saw her, standing between a man's arms, there beneath the upper catwalk, right outside the cell.

The wall was half-open, somehow, probably a result of the damage we'd taken in the tunnel.

"There you are," said Alphonse, holding her. "I was wondering what took you so long."

He had a gash on his forehead, with blood streaming down his cheek, and I spotted a body behind him. It could only be Docker.

"Alphonse, what did you do?" I asked.

"I took care of a problem," he answered. "Docker was trying to hurt the girl, but I stopped him. Now, she's safe." He moved his arm off of her shoulder and she came running to me. "I need to sit down now, if you don't mind."

He stumbled backwards, into a crate, wavering for a second.

I looked at Lex. "Did the other one try to hurt you?"

She nodded. "Yeah, it was scary."

"Hey, go upstairs, okay? Go wait with Octavia for me."

She ran to the stairs and took off. I pulled out my pistol, just in case this whole thing was a trap, and edged my way over to the cell, trying to get a better look at Docker.

"He's dead. I made certain," said Alphonse. His eyes were swirling, like he was about to pass out.

"What happened to you?" I asked.

He smirked. "Took a hit from a pipe," he answered. "Really, Captain, you should get your plumbing looked at. There's far too many loose pipes around here."

Then, he passed out.

* * *

"Holy shit," said Abigail as she entered the cargo bay and saw the dead body.

"I know," I said, crossing my arms.

Freddie was right behind her, an equal look of shock on his face. "What happened? Is he okay?"

"No, he's not okay, Freddie. He's dead."

"How? And what's with the other one?" He pointed to the second floor, where Alphonse was lying on a table.

"He's fine, just unconscious," said Octavia, sitting beside him.

I'd moved him, since Octavia couldn't climb the stairs.

"What happened?" asked Freddie.

"Siggy, play the audio," I said.

There was a short pause, followed by a light click, and then the recording played, beginning with a long stretch of silence, followed by some static and what could only be hard turbulence from our impact inside the slip tunnel.

A worried voice, unsteady and frantic, quivered as the loud tearing and banging continued. "What's going on?!"

Another voice answered, much calmer and in control. "Perhaps we're under attack."

"Is it the Union?" asked the frightened voice, which was becoming clearer now. "Don't they know we're onboard?"

"If General Brigham attacked this ship, we would have been destroyed by now. It must be someone else."

"Brigham wouldn't do that, would he?"

"It doesn't matter, Docker. Just don't think about it."

"What? Why would you say that?"

"The Union probably assumes we're dead. Even if they found out we're prisoners, they wouldn't put any value on our lives...not compared to the mission."

"You're just saying that because you've been giving these people information. I'm not some traitor like you. They'll come for me."

"You're being stupid. No one cares about you, aside from your family. We're just pawns in all this."

"And you're a coward," he countered.

"That's funny, you calling me that. I seem to remember we both surrendered, back on our ship."

"At least I tried to escape when I had the chance. You just sat in this room."

"And you failed, I seem to recall. You can't—" Another hard burst of turbulence interrupted him.

"I need to get out of here!" exclaimed Docker. He started banging on the wall. "Gods, let me out! Let me out!"

"Stop, you idiot!" said Alphonse. "There's no point in yelling. You can't get that door open from in here!"

"I have to!" he shouted. "I have to get out and talk to the General! He'll help me!"

"General Brigham doesn't care about you!" said Alphonse.

"Yes, he does! He's a war hero!" he shouted. "All I have to is...all I have to do is get that girl back!"

"Would you listen to yourself? You're talking about escaping a locked room and getting off of a ship with no plan, despite the armed personnel and—"

"Shut up! Shut up or I'll kill you right here!" yelled Docker. He was sounding more hysterical by the moment. "I can't handle this! I just want to go home...I want to get back to my wife! I just want—"

A series of rapid tearing and banging sounds exploded through my earpiece, the loudest yet. It lasted for several seconds before finally going quiet.

"The-The door!" yelled Docker.

"It's open?" asked Alphonse.

"Help me with it! We can get it the rest of the way if we—"

"Docker, stop, you're going to get yourself killed if you start running through this ship!"

"I have to get out!" he shouted. A screeching noise, like metal sliding against metal. "Help me, Alphonse!"

It took them some time to open it, but we kept listening through the grinding and the screeching, despite how ear-piercingly awful it was.

"Docker, hold on a second. Let's think this through. If you leave, you'll only run into the crew, and you already know the captain isn't afraid to shoot you."

"I'll get on the shuttle and run. It's right down the hall above us. If we hurry, we can steal it. We just need a way out of—"

He suddenly stopped talking.

"What are you doing?" asked Lex in a curious voice. In all the commotion, neither had seen her coming, not until she was already in the cargo bay.

"I-It's the girl," muttered Docker. "Alphonse, it's her!"

"I see that," said Alphonse.

"H-Hey, little one, are you doing okay?" asked Docker.

"Um...yeah, I'm okay. Are you? Why is the door broken?"

"Don't worry about that," he answered. "Is anyone else around?"

"Yeah, Octavia is upstairs. She's fixing something."

"Oh, uh, that's good. Can you help me out?"

"Docker, stop it," whispered Alphonse. "Are you trying to get yourself killed? If any of the crew sees you talking to her, they'll kill you on the spot."

"Hey, come here," he said, ignoring Alphonse. "We can't see you from over there."

"Um, I don't think I'm supposed to," said Lex.

"No, it's okay. We're friends of the Captain's," said Docker.

"Oh, um, really?"

Footsteps as she grew closer. "That's right, it's okay."

"Stay back, girl!" ordered Alphonse. "Don't come any—"

The recording stopped, cutting him off. Abigail and Freddie both looked at me, confused. "Is that it?" asked Fred.

"Seems so," I said.

Sigmond chimed in. "Internal devices ceased to function properly at this time. I apologize for the inconvenience."

"What does Lex say about it?" asked Freddie.

"She told me the two of them started fighting, beat on each

other, and then Alphonse got the upper hand. That was only about twenty seconds before I got here, best I can tell."

"I don't get it," said Freddie. "Why did Alphonse stop him from taking Lex?"

Abigail looked at me. "He knew we'd kill him if he tried."

I nodded. "In a heartbeat. Besides, he didn't know Siggy was having problems with the ship, or even what the turbulence was from, so maybe he figured taking the shuttle wouldn't work. Siggy has protocols to stop that from happening, unless I authorize it."

"I guess that makes sense," muttered Freddie.

"Either way, we'll question him when he's awake," I said.

Freddie stared at the body. "What do we do with him in the meantime?"

"We're still in slipspace for another hour," I said.

"Space him now," said Abigail, flatly. "That's the only option for him."

"Are we sure about that?" asked Freddie.

"She's right," I said. "It's what he deserves."

I helped the two of them pick him up and carry him. We wrapped him in a sheet and made sure Lex was in her room before taking him to the airlock. After placing him inside, I had Siggy open the hatch, releasing him into the slip tunnel.

They say when you release a body into slipspace, its atoms are destroyed and reformed into new energy. Scientists believe that the walls are in a constant state of nuclear fusion and fission, creating and destroying atoms on a constant loop. Some scientists think this is part of the reason it looks the way it does, but no one has been able to explain why or how it happens, only that it does.

Regardless, we sent Docker's corpse into the stream, letting it float and collide with the inner wall, disintegrating upon impact. In less than a moment, his body ceased to exist. The truest form of death I could imagine.

TWENTY

After sending Docker's body into the slipstream, I wanted to turn my attention to the only remaining prisoner in my possession. However, Alphonse was incapacitated at the moment, which meant that would have to wait.

I gave Freddie a gun and told him to stay with both our resident cripple and the ensign. Even if Fred couldn't shoot straight, Octavia was there with her own weapon, ready to kill if it came to it.

As for me and Abigail, we returned to the bridge right as the ship arrived at the next S.G. Point. Without missing a beat, I took us into the new tunnel, beginning the final slip towards our destination.

Abigail had the star chart up, examining our route. "It looks like we'll pass over where we need to go," she said.

"How's that?" I asked.

"The tunnel is two lightyears too long. We'll need to turn around, once we arrive."

"Turn around? Without a slip tunnel, it would take us days to get there."

"It's the only option we have," she said, giving me a light shrug.

"Meanwhile, we've got two armies after us, an unconscious prisoner, and a ship full of problems."

"One thing at a time," she said.

Abigail and I spent the next twenty minutes going over damage reports from each of the ship's systems. From what I could tell, most of it was superficial, with some slight damage to the hull, cargo bay gate, and internal sensors. No serious problems with the atmospheric systems, weapons, or the engines, thank the gods.

I considered going back to check on Alphonse when Siggy's voice came over the com. "Sir, we have a slight problem with our flight path. It's—" Before he could say anything else the swirling green of the screen in front of me suddenly changed, reshaping to form the dark, black void of normal space. "—broken," he finally finished.

"What just happened?" asked Abigail.

"As I was saying, internal scans of the tunnel showed that this slip gap point was prematurely formed," said Sigmond.

"You mean this tunnel was cut in half?" I asked. "How the shit does that even happen?"

"Unknown, sir. However, it would seem we have arrived at our final destination."

"Hold on, you mean that breach in the tunnel took us—"

"He's right," Abigail said, pulling up the star chart. "Look here. This is where the tunnel was supposed to take us—" She followed the line with her finger, then pulled it back. "—and instead, we're here, right at the end of the original line."

"The map still shows the tunnel going further out," I observed.

"It must be outdated," she said.

"Siggy, why did this happen?" I asked.

"It could be artificial, based on the instability of the current rift. However—"

"Artificial?" asked Abigail. "Is he saying that rift isn't supposed to be there? That someone put it there?"

"I've heard of these," I muttered. "People talk about breaks in the tunnels. They say they're not supposed to be there, like someone dropped a bomb inside and tore open a new hole. I always thought it was bullshit, like the guys who say they've seen the gods sitting at the far end of the galaxy. You know, real kooky shit."

"Sir, if you'll allow me to continue," said Sigmond.

"Oh, sorry, pal. I thought you were done."

"Think nothing of it, sir," he said. "As I was saying, the new rift could be artificial. However, the tunnel appeared to be intact when we entered it. I performed a long range internal scan of the tunnel and found that it would take us approximately two hours to reach the next S.G. Point."

"In other words, that rift wasn't there when we went into the tunnel," I said.

"Correct."

"What do you think that means?" I asked, looking at Abigail.

"Maybe it reacted to us, somehow," she said.

We both sat there in silence for a minute, trying to put together what just happened. "Could it be something about the ship?" I finally asked.

"It could," she said, "or it couldn't. How do we find out?"

"I don't know. Maybe we don't."

Abigail shook her head. "Sigmond, can you scan the system and show us where we are, specifically? Give me a detailed map of the area."

"Working," said the A.I. "Analysis complete."

The holo display changed to show a binary star system. Six planets, twelve moons.

"Are any of these planets habitable?" asked Abigail.

No answer.

"Sigmond?"

"Apologies, madam. I was attempting a deep scan of one of the planets, which at first appeared incapable of sustaining life, but it seems I was mistaken."

"So, it's habitable?" I asked.

"Only a small portion, but I have no explanation for it. There is an area, twelve kilometers in radius, where the atmosphere is breathable."

"So, there's a circle of land where we can breathe?" asked Abigail.

"A three-dimensional semi-circle, by point of fact," explained Sigmond. "It ends on the ground and extends two hundred meters at the center."

"What the hell?" I muttered. "Is it some kind of colony?"

"There is no indication of colonization. I detect no humans or architecture."

I leaned in to examine the circle. It was in the center of a spot of land near the middle of a continent. Nothing was particularly noteworthy about it, other than the fact that this existed. I'd never seen anything like it.

"And the atmosphere outside of whatever this is?" asked Abigail.

"Highly toxic," answered Sigmond.

I couldn't help but balk at all of this. "First we're taken out of a slipspace tunnel without warning; now we're looking at two atmospheres on a single planet, with no apparent reason. What the fuck is going on today?"

"It seems the closer we get to our goal, the more out-of-the-ordinary things become," said Abigail.

"Siggy, list the contents of the atmosphere outside this so-called habitable zone," I said, leaning closer to the dash.

Instantly, the display changed, showing a detailed list of the planet's makeup.

95.31% carbon dioxide

1.91% argon

1.58% nitrogen

0.974% oxygen

0. 226% carbon monoxide

I glanced over the numbers. *Yep, totally unlivable,* I thought. You wouldn't catch on fire from contact, but you'd sure as shit suffocate.

"Now, show the readout for the habitable portion," said Abigail.

The screen changed and another list appeared, only this time was drastically different.

78.09% nitrogen

20.95% oxygen

0.93% argon

0.04% carbon dioxide

0.002% neon

0.0005% helium

0.00018% methane

"That looks much better," said Abigail.

I scratched my head. "Why do you think it's segmented like that?"

"You're asking me?"

"I'm asking anyone. You just happened to be here," I said.

She ignored my jab. "It can't be natural, can it? There's no way a bubble of breathable air just forms on a planet for no reason. Someone had to *put* it there. Sigmond, do you see anything artificial down there? Any signs of human technology?"

"Initial scans revealed none. However, I can perform a deep scan of the planet and provide more in-depth information."

"Go ahead, please" said Abigail.

"Please stand by. This may take several moments."

I got on my feet, continuing to stare at the planet sitting before us. My eyes found the continent where the circle was, and it didn't take me long to spot the little green dot. It was small, though not so much you couldn't see it, since it was surrounded by brown.

A little piece of life at the center of a wasteland.

* * *

Hitchens met me in the lounge. If anyone could help us figure out this mess, I figured it was him.

"Gracious, I really couldn't say, Captain," he said, staring at the pad I'd given him, which contained all the data we'd collected so far on the planet.

"Fucking seriously Professor?"

He raised his finger. "Doctor."

"You need to give me something better than that," I said.

He examined the data again, scratching his ear. "You say the tunnel opened prematurely?"

"That's right."

"And we have no idea why, except that it reacted to us?"

"Also right."

He thought for a moment. "Could it be that it is something we have with us, rather than the ship, itself?"

"You mean our cargo?" I asked, trying to think of something that might be a match. "What about those artifacts of yours?"

"Ah!" he exclaimed, tapping his nose. "Now, there's an idea!"

"You think so?" I asked.

"Could be, yes, could be! Oh, but," he frowned, "without traveling back into the tunnel, we won't be able to test it. Speaking of which, have you tried to reopen the rift? What happens if we can't get it open again?"

"Slow down, Hitchens. You're getting way too far ahead of yourself. What about those artifacts?"

"Ah, yes, I apologize." He cleared his throat. "Little Lex was with me during the rupture. We were playing with the cube that your friend, the teenage girl from the mining town gave you. Now, what was the name of that city?"

"Spiketown," I reminded him. "The girl's name was Camilla."

"Camilla!" he exclaimed, happily. "Such a nice family, those two. Her and her father. Bolin, was it?"

"Let's reminisce later," I said, trying to pull his attention back to what actually mattered. "This artifact, what did it do?"

"Ah, well, it was actually rather similar to the one that injured poor Lex's hand."

"Did this one do the same? Is she okay?" I asked.

"Oh, she's perfectly fine, Captain. I tried to stop her from playing with it, but she's so fast at her age, it's hard for me to keep up."

"What did it do when she touched it?"

"It activated a beam, the same as the other one, although it seemed to do nothing of note. I suspected it might simply be an artificial light source. Perhaps a toy of some kind."

"Seems to me it's more than that. Where's Lex? And where's the box?"

The answer to both, I learned, was in a bedroom down the hall. I found her fast asleep, sprawled out like wild animal. She must have been exhausted from everything that happened in the cargo bay, or maybe it was just the highs and lows of being a kid. Watching Alphonse kill Docker had to be stressful, but she'd been through worse since I met her.

I sat on the side of the bed and nudged her with my knuckles. "Kid," I said, bluntly. "Hey, kid."

She squirmed, clawing the pillow with her fingers, like she was reaching for something, and then went back to her original position.

I tapped her forehead with my index finger. "Hey, you little razorbeast. Wake up."

She cracked her eyes and I could tell she'd been dreaming, just by the look on her face. It was like she'd been someplace else, far away from here. "Huh...? Mr. Hughes?"

"Hey, kid. You doing okay?"

She nodded, flinging her head up and down like she'd just had a burst of energy, and smiled.

"I wanted to ask you where that box you were playing with went to."

"Huh?" she said. "Oh, the box!" She turned and reached beneath the pillow, inside the gap between the bed and wall. "It fell down here."

I watched her pull it up with both hands, scratching the paint on the wall in the process, though I didn't say anything. After a second, she handed it to me with a wide grin on her face. "This is it?" I asked.

She nodded. "Yeah, that's the one Mr. Hitchens gave me to play with."

"Think I can borrow it for a little bit?"

"Yeah!" she exclaimed. "Are you gonna play, too?"

I gave her a pat on the head. "Sure, kid. As soon as I figure out what the hell it does."

* * *

I was on my way back to the cockpit with Hitchens when Siggy informed me that Alphonse was awake. "Tell Octavia I'm on my way."

I told Hitchens to come with me so we might have a chance to figure out what was going on with this box. I took a deep breath as I thought about the day I was having. One thing at a time, I heard Abigail's voice say inside my head. One thing at a time.

Alphonse was sitting up on the table with a patch over his forehead, looking dazed and half-asleep. It was a similar look to the one Lex had had only a few moments ago. "Welcome to the party," said Freddie as Hitchens and I entered the upper deck of the cargo bay.

"How's he doing?" I asked Octavia.

"Better, but he's got a cracked skull. I've already applied some medi-gel, but that will take a few days to heal."

"You hear that, Alphonse?" I asked.

He looked at me, blinking. "R-Right."

I whistled. "Oh, yeah. He's messed up bad."

"He'll be fine, as I said," remarked Octavia. She swiveled in her chair to face Hitchens. "How's Lex doing?"

He approached her side and placed a hand on the arm of her chair. "She's tired herself out. We left her resting in Ms. Pryar's room."

I leaned in closer to Alphonse. "Hey, you and I need to have a conversation."

"A...conversation?" he asked, trying to focus on my face.

I nodded. "About a few things, if you think you can handle it."

He held the side of his head. "Your nurse here has me on some kind of—"

"Not a nurse," interjected Octavia.

"—some kind of painkillers. I'm not sure...what, exactly, but...they're definitely working." His voice was suddenly wavering, like he could barely keep the words together.

"You stuck him full of drugs?" I asked.

Octavia shrugged. "I had to do something. He kept screaming when I tried to sew the wound."

Alphonse started to close his eyes.

"Hey!" I snapped my fingers in front of his eyes. "Wake up, you idiot!"

He blinked, rapidly. "Sorry! I'm just so tired."

"Before you pass out, tell me what happened with Docker," I said.

"He tried to hurt the girl, and I..." He closed his eyes, briefly, then reopened them. "I...don't know."

"You don't know?"

"I didn't want to do it. He was right. We could've left. Taken the shuttle. Ran away. Stole the girl. She's valuable. I couldn't do it, though. She's just a child. I..."

His eyelids drooped, and he began to waver where he sat. I took his shoulders and helped him lie down again. "Easy," I said.

"Sorry," he muttered, right as his back touched the table.

"One last thing," I said, staring down at him.

He gave me a slight nod, and I could see the tiredness in his eyes. "Okay."

"Who are you?" I asked. "And I want the truth about it."

He took a long and steady breath, like he was savoring the air, like it was something to cherish, and exhaled it back out, licking his lips. "I'm Alphonse," he finally answered. "An ensign in the Union Fleet."

I sighed. "Not this again. I know there's more to—"

"And I'm also a member of the Constables."

My eyes suddenly widened at the sound of the term. The Constables. The assassin spies of the Union. I'd never encountered one before, not up close, never in-person. Not many had, the way I heard it. Constables were a secret arm of the government, sent to deal with every major threat in the known galaxy. They went where the Union couldn't, drifting like ghosts in a field, never seen, but always there. Always watching.

I took a step back.

"Did he..." Freddie's mouth hung open. "Did he just say he was a Constable?"

"I believe he did," said Hitchens.

I stared down at Alphonse. His breathing had changed to a different cadence, indicating sleep. "Holy shit," I finally managed to say. "Holy shit almighty."

Twenty-One

"What kind of drugs do you have?" I asked, standing beside the table where Alphonse was lying.

"We managed to pick up a healthy supply at the station," informed Octavia. "What kind do you want?"

"Something to keep him knocked out for a while," I said.

"He has a head injury. I wouldn't advise giving him any opiates right now, unless you want to risk putting him into a coma," she said.

"I don't want to leave you here alone with him," I said. "What if he wakes up and tries something? He's a goddamn Constable."

"You or Abigail could simply stand guard beside me," she said.

I shook my head. "We have another job."

She and Hitchens exchanged looks. "What job?" asked Hitchens.

"Did you already forget about the planet outside? We have to act now if we're going to beat the Sarkonians and the Union. If they figure out where we are, I want to be gone before they show up."

"Oh! Of course, Captain," said Hitchens. "Pardon my ignorance."

"It's fine," I said, tapping his shoulder. "We just need to figure out exactly what the fuck is down there and why that map of yours brought us here."

"What about me?" asked Freddie.

"Someone has to stay with Octavia, just in case she needs help with Alphonse."

"You think because I'm in this chair I can't kick an ass or two?" asked Octavia.

"Are you kidding? I have no doubt you could take down a dozen guys if they came at you, but someone has to watch your back."

She looked at Freddie. "We'll hold down the ship until everyone returns, then, won't we?"

He nodded. "Yes, ma'am."

"Remember," I said, "you need to keep Alphonse contained. Even though he saved Lex from Docker, he still works for the Union."

"Speaking of Lex, what are we doing with her?" asked Freddie.

"What do you mean?" I said.

"Should we keep her up here with..." He paused, glancing at the unconscious Constable on our table. "...this man?"

"She should be fine as long as the two of you stay on your guard," I said.

"Actually, Captain, if I might," interjected Hitchens.

"You have a better idea?" I asked.

He nodded. "Lex has the ability to activate the artifacts. It may behoove us to involve her in our expedition. If we encounter another atlas or a Cartographer, such as we did back on Epsilon, we may want her by our side."

I considered what he was suggesting. Hitchens always had a talent for helping me to see the logical solution. "That makes sense," I said, after a second.

"Besides," he added with a smile. "She's been aching to go outdoors. Imagine the joy it would bring her."

* * *

I decided to go with Hitchens' suggestion and let Lex join us on the surface, not because she wanted to be outside. No, I wasn't as sentimental as the good doctor. I just knew the safest place for her to be was by my side, where I could keep an eye on her. The same was true for the rest of my crew, but circumstances prevented that from happening right now, which meant I had to pick and choose.

Abigail, Lex, Hitchens, and I boarded the shuttle and set a course for the semicircle of habitable atmosphere on the planet's surface. It was a twenty-minute flight, although it felt much longer. The little ship rattled and shook as we entered the heavy atmosphere of the toxic section of the planet. I asked everyone to gear up in proper spacesuits, including Lex, who needed help getting into hers. I'd managed to buy a child's sized suit while we were visiting the hospital, only a few days before this.

I could tell Lex was excited. Her eyes lit up as she watched us tear through the clouds and brown gas, slowly entering the lower section of the sky. "I wonder if there's any animals," she said, trying to catch a look at the valley below us, although it was too far out of view.

"No lifeforms were detected, upon early scans," said Sigmond.

"Nu-uh," she told him. "There still could be some."

"Highly unlikely," said Sigmond.

"What do you know, Siggy? You don't have eyes."

"While true, my sensors are capable of observing a wide spectrum that far exceeds that of—"

"Both of you stop arguing," I said.

"Siggy started it," said Lex, trying to give me a pouty face.

The ship suddenly vibrated and I saw a flash outside the window. "What was that?" asked Abigail.

"It would seem we have passed through an electromagnetic field and into the habitable region of the planet," informed Sigmond.

"A field?" I asked, looking outside. The sky was still brown and cloudy, but the air closer to us was thinner, less congested. "Are you saying this pocket is protected by a force field?"

"Unknown, sir," said Sigmond. "I was unable to detect it from orbit."

"Unable? Why not?"

"Unknown," he repeated.

"Does that mean the rest of his scans were useless?" asked Abigail.

"Could be," I said. If Siggy couldn't tell us what was on the surface of this place, then we could be walking into anything. "We'll have to be ready."

Abigail gripped her rifle with both hands. "Way ahead of you."

We touched down a moment later, waiting a few seconds for the hull to decompress while the coolant kicked in. In the meantime, I secured my helmet and checked my suit's seals, telling the others to do the same. When we were finally ready to go, I slammed the release button near the gate, unlocking the clamp. The door cracked, and a beam of light shined through, hitting Hitchens' knees and growing.

As the door continued to open, I could see the excitement on Lex's face as she bobbed on each foot, ready to run. Hitchens held her hand, making sure she didn't just run out blindly into the field. We'd secure the area first, long before she left the ship.

The sky outside was slightly overcast with clouds, a brown tint, mixed with shades of red, but none of that seemed to stop the two suns from shining their warm light on us. It felt nice against my cheeks, even through the tinted visor, and I had to admit I liked it.

I checked the thermometer to find it was 30.05 degrees. Hot, but not so much that you couldn't stand it.

Abigail kept the anxious Lex by her side, right on the edge of the shuttle's gate, which had dropped into the soft dirt and thick, green grass.

The readout of the atmosphere indicated that the air was breathable, just as Siggy had suggested.

87.084% nitrogen

2.946% oxygen

0.934% argon

0.04% carbon dioxide

0.001818% neon

0.000524% helium

0.000179% methane

So Sigmond's readings were correct, at least as far the atmosphere inside this bubble went. Why he couldn't detect the field around it was anyone's guess. Could that mean his scans had been mostly right? Or had we simply gotten lucky with the atmosphere?

I supposed we'd find out soon.

"Is it safe?" asked Abigail.

"Looks like it," I said. "Let's keep our suits on for now, just in case. This place doesn't make sense, so we should probably stay cautious."

"Agreed," she said.

"I can't take the suit off?" asked Lex.

"Not here. It's too risky," said Abigail.

Lex frowned, slightly, and nodded. "Okay."

I touched the screen on my wrist, activating the planet's map. A holo formed above my arm, lighting up in a flash to show me a three-dimensional recreation. Using my two fingers, I touched the floating orb and zoomed in on our present location, revealing the circle. Another zoom, and I had our position. "It looks like we're a kilometer away from the center of this, which is weird since I asked Sigmond to land us as close as possible."

"Apologies, sir. I don't know what happened. I input the proper coordinates, based on your suggestions," said the A.I. "This is most perplexing."

"It's not a long walk," said Abigail. "We can do that in ten-minutes. Five if we hurry."

"Let's get going," I said, waving them on.

The valley's grass grew thinner as we walked. I could see the dirt between the blades, hard and cracked, like the salt flats of a dry desert. By the time we reached the middle of the circle, we were nearly out of the grass altogether, though there were still patches of it. I was surprised there were no trees here, not to mention rivers or lakes. The more we walked toward the east, the brown began to overtake the green.

Soon, it would be nothing but desert sand and dry stone.

* * *

Hitchens spotted it first.

A structure in the distance, big enough to see from far away. It looked like a round building, broken in places and ragged, although we'd need to get closer to see for sure.

The heat was beginning to grow stronger, perhaps because we'd entered a drier area. I checked my thermometer and saw that, yes, the temperature had risen nearly two degrees. No wonder I was sweating my ass off. If it got any worse, we might have to turn back.

I glanced directly above us, expecting to see one or both of the suns towering overhead. It felt like noon on this planet, but instead, I only saw the moon. Strange, that it should be so big or out in the daylight when it was so bright out.

The bright sunlight forced me to look down after a few seconds. I activated my visor's tint to keep it dimmer.

When we were no more than a hundred meters away, we began to see strange rocks, half-sunk in the ground.

They had markings—etched lines on their sides, almost like the relics Hitchens had on the ship. The jolly doctor picked one up to examine it, turning it in his hands, studying it. He had fascination in his eyes, and I saw the sparkle of a man in his element, in the place he belonged.

"Look at the way the lines are engraved," he said, following the lines with his finger. "It's reminiscent of the ruins we found on Epsilon."

"The Cartographer?" I asked, remembering the walk we took to reach the mountain, discovering the ruins beneath it, the buried technology that came to life when Lex found her way into that chair, and the animals that came afterwards. There was so much I didn't understand about all this. The stone he had looked nothing like the relics, not to me and my untrained mind...but Hitchens— he had an eye for this. He saw the connections that I just couldn't make.

"See here," he said, motioning for me to get closer. He touched the indentation in it, following the line until it looped into a circle. "This is the same pattern as the Cartographer. It was all over Epsilon's ruins."

"Can I touch it?" asked Lex, who was standing just a meter away. She ogled the stone, a strange curiosity in her eyes.

"Of course, my dear," said Hitchens, handing it to her, gently.

The moment she touched it, the markings began to glow a strange blue, as did her tattoos. She smiled as the light hit her cheeks with a soft glow. "Pretty," she whispered, staring into the stone.

We all watched with some reverence, having no explanation for what we were seeing. Somehow, this little stone on this remote planet in the middle of nowhere had a connection with this quirky albino girl. What that was, none of us could've told you, but it was evident, here in this moment, that we had come to the right place.

Twenty-Two

The rocks were sparse at first, but grew more abundant the further we walked, and soon I saw the object that had once been their home.

A building, round and tall, although I could only barely make out the design, and I really couldn't tell you what it was. Not even when we were there, right outside the broken wall, staring up at it in awe.

It seemed to have a tube behind it that stretched up into the sky. Round and thin, with cables coming from the ground, firmly strapped to the tube's sides. It continued on into the sky, far out of view, heading into the gas of the other atmosphere, disappearing into the horizon, as though it went on forever.

"What in heavens could this be?" asked Abigail, once we were close enough to see it.

Despite how close we were, I still couldn't say. The building was round and had a hole in the middle, like a donut. There were markings on it, the same as the stones in the sand, and they formed strange glyphs all across the walls.

"What do you think it means?" I asked, looking at Hitchens for answers.

He had none to give. "I wish I knew, Captain."

At the center of this structure, we found a small building, half decayed and falling in on itself. Behind it, I saw what appeared to be a track, or the start of one, and it continued on into the tube, which began here and went up into the sky. There were no vehicles here, no transport to board so that you could ride the railway. Not that we would, of course, given how little we knew of it, but I could tell this was something made to travel on. At least, that's how it looked to me, but what did I know? Not as much as I thought, I was quickly realizing.

I walked closer to the tube's opening, which was far larger than me, and dark inside. "This is some ominous shit," I muttered, turning back around to look at my crew.

"A fitting description, if ever I heard one," said Hitchens, leaning so far into the tube that I thought he might fall into it.

"Look at this building," said Abigail, still holding Lex's hand. "What do you think it is?"

I approached the structure and examined the cracked walls. By the look of it, I guessed this thing was only a fraction of its original size, which must have been several stories tall at one point. The bulk of the tower was covered in its own corpse, surrounded by fallen debris and no doors to speak of.

I checked the map, bringing the holo up on my wrist. According to the readout, we were directly in the center of the circle, although I saw nothing on the map to indicate that this tower (or any of this) was actually here. Another sign that the sensors had been unable to penetrate the atmospheric shield.

A sudden chill ran over me as I quickly realized that I actually had no fucking idea what was on this planet, and I didn't just mean the buildings.

The fallen tower had walls like all the rest. Only more markings along the stones, broken and cut off. Lex wanted to get closer, but I told Abigail to keep her back.

"Captain, look at this," said Hitchens. His voice pulled me out of my thoughts. He was standing near the back corner of the building with his hand on a piece of stone. "I believe there's something here."

I went to him, looking at the wall he had his hand on, only to discover that the stone wasn't actually part of it. This was a separate piece, or perhaps it had broken off some time ago. Either way, it was loose, and maybe it meant a way inside. "Help me with this," I said, gripping the edge.

He did, and together we pulled, heaving until we had it sliding back. We both moved out of its way as the rock tipped and fell into the sand, slamming with a heavy thud. "Very good," wheezed Hitchens, already out of breath. "Very good, indeed."

The hole in the wall was large enough for a smaller person than myself. Abigail, maybe, and certainly Lex, although I wouldn't let the girl go first. "Think you can squeeze in, Abby?"

"I believe so," she said, looking it over.

"Do be careful now," suggested Hitchens.

She eased inside, and I ducked to try and get a better look. Abigail went slowly, staying mindful of the rocks so she didn't compromise the suit.

"What do you see?" called Hitchens.

I watched her climb up a fallen wall, trying to leverage herself to reach the other side. "The same thing you see out there," she managed to say, once she had her feet planted again.

"That's a pity," Hitchens said, looking at me.

"Wait!" Abigail yelled, and it hurt my ear, since her voice was coming through the com inside my helmet. She was out of my line-of-sight, too, having disappeared behind more debris. "There's something here, beneath the ground. I can see it through the cracks. It looks like glass and—" She paused. "—perhaps some metal wiring. I'm not certain."

"Don't these suits use cameras?" Hitchens asked, looking at me.

Oh, yeah, I thought, slightly embarrassed that I hadn't remembered something so obvious. I decided to blame it on being completely distracted by the standing tower in the middle of a self-contained, habitable atmosphere on a planet in the middle of bum-fuck nowhere. "Good thinking," I said. "Siggy, activate Abby's suitcam and feed it to us."

"Activating now," said Sigmond.

The feed appeared in the upper left corner of my visor, showing Abby's perspective as she dug through some fist-sized stones. Behind them, a small hole that seemed to drop into the basement of whatever this tower was. "Are you seeing this, Doc?"

"Most certainly!" answered Hitchens. I could hear the curious excitement in his voice. It was the sound of a man on the edge of his seat, watching something he considered remarkable unfold before him. "Careful, Ms. Pryar! You'll want to mind the walls there."

"I have it," she said, removing another rock. "Can you see inside yet?"

"Hold your head steady for a second," I said.

She paused. "Like this?"

"Good. Can you activate your light? The one on your wrist."

She messed around with her armpad, briefly, and then a steady light appeared. She aimed her arm towards the hole, keeping herself as steady as possible so Hitchens and I could observe. "How's that?"

There was glass, as she had said, but it was curved like a bowl that had been turned upside down. Beneath it, long tubes ran throughout, with no indication as to their purpose or direction. It was like some kind of machine, but none that I'd ever seen. "Perfect," I said. "Hitchens, how about it? See anything?"

"Oh, my," he muttered. "Oh, my, oh, my, would you look at that?"

"Talk, dammit," I said. "Stop rambling."

"I've seen architecture like that before," he answered.

"Where? You mean back on Epsilon?" I asked.

"Not quite," he said. "The pictures I saw were recovered by the Church's founder many decades ago."

"You mean that Darrel guy?"

"Darius," he corrected. "Yes, Darius Clare. I believe one of the images he unearthed looked similar to what we are seeing now."

"Was there anything else?" I asked.

"There were several, but it's been a long while since I saw them. Oh, perhaps Frederick could assist us!"

"How's that?"

"He's on the ship, so he could transmit them, and he has some experience with the research."

Less than a minute later, I had Freddie with me on the com. "Think you can find something?" I asked, once Hitchens explained the situation.

"I think so," he said.

"That doesn't sound very confident," I said.

"Sorry, just a second. I need to get my pad. Sigmond, can you transmit my screen to their suits?" asked Freddie. I could hear him breathing rapidly as he ran through the ship. I had to give him credit. He was motivated.

"Certainly," said Siggy.

I heard some rustling and bumbling on the other side of the

line as Freddie hurried to get his pad. "Here, I think. No, wait. Yes! Here it is."

An image appeared on my visor. It looked similar, as Hitchens had suggested, although it wasn't the same. This one was surrounded by metal, with fair lighting and clean, no signs of dust or rubble. The architecture around it, while not exactly the same, had identical glyphs and markings, meaning there had to be some kind of connection. What it might be, I couldn't say, but it was enough to suggest we were on the right path.

The right path. The words echoed in my head. Was that even accurate? How could I know what the right path was when nothing about it had made sense? In what way did any of this connect back to Earth? From what I could tell, sitting here in front of this wreck of a tower, the answer was that it didn't.

What could be missing? What piece did we need to connect the dots?

I heard a rustling sound nearby.

I started to look down when suddenly the glyphs on the wall lit up, shining a bold cerulean blue. I looked down to see Lex standing there, a wide smile on her face and her open palm on the stone.

Abigail shrieked inside, and Hitchens nearly stumbled back. "Holy!"

I started to say something when the ground shook and I bent my knees. The light on the wall grew brighter at once.

I grabbed Lex by the arm and pulled her away. "Everyone move! Abby get out of there!"

I saw the light fill from within the monument, building to the top and—

A sudden burst exploded from the top of the tower, shooting a single beam of light into the sky. It pierced the clouds, splitting them apart, and went straight into—

Into the moon. The same moon that hadn't moved since we'd arrived, floating 45 degrees from where I was standing.

The beam struck it somewhere near the equator, and the light expanded quickly, immediately, like electricity in a power grid.

I watched with awe as the moon went from a dead ball of rock to something more. Something mechanical, technological, sophisticated. Why had our sensors not detected this earlier? What was it about this place?

"Holy shit!" yelled Abigail and she threw herself out of the hole in the wall. She clawed to escape, trying to dig her way out. I reached for her, grabbing her hand and pulling.

She stumbled out of the wall right as the beam died, yet the lines on the wall continued to shine. "What just happened?!"

I pointed to the sky. "See for yourself."

Her eyes widened when she saw it. "What in the gods' names is that?"

"It's a moon!" exclaimed Lex, smiling.

"It sure is," I muttered, tilting my head to stare up at it. Of all the things I'd seen today, from rupturing slip tunnels to a pocket atmosphere, I had to admit that a glowing moon topped it all.

"Oh, my goodness," said Hitchens. His voice surprised me. I'd nearly forgotten he was there. "Frederick, are you also seeing this?"

"I am!" Fred's voice buzzed with crackling static. "It looks like...couldn't say for...have Sigmond run a...need to scan."

"What was that?" I asked.

"...aptain? Hello? You're...can't get..."

"It could be interference from this structure," said Hitchens, motioning to the glowing tower beside us.

"Or the giant moon thing hovering over our heads," I said.

"Or whatever that tube is," added Abigail, looking behind me at the tunnel. "Uh, Jace."

"What?" I asked.

She pointed. "Something's happening."

I turned toward the tube entrance to see that it was now lit up inside. Not only that, but the platform in front of it was moving.

The platform pulled apart and an object came rising out of the ground, a vessel of some sort, sleek and black, like a long triangle.

Before I could say anything, a door opened along the leftmost side of the triangle, releasing steam into the air, and the area around it became illuminated.

"What in the world?" asked Hitchens.

The ground beneath me began to shake, and I turned around

to see the tower caving in on itself. "Get back!" I shouted.

The three of them ran toward me, closer to the ship and railway. The tower's walls cracked, breaking and crumbling, chunks of stone snapping off and falling to the hard dirt. Suddenly, the entire east wall fell away like water, sliding free of the rest, sending dirt and dust towards us. We covered our visors and looked away.

More noise followed as the rest of the tower caved, all of it falling into the underground, creating a large hole and opening the place Abigail had found before. Now, there was a blue glow coming from inside, and I could see the machine turning, spinning, rotating. The light continued to build, growing brighter with the passing seconds.

"It's all falling!" yelled Abigail.

She was right. The ground around the hole was breaking, snapping off into the inner sanctum. The hole was expanding, and quickly.

"We need to get out of here!" I shouted.

We started to run towards the exit but a divide split along the ground. We stopped, suddenly, and Hitchens nearly slammed into it.

The crack expanded toward him. I grabbed the back of his collar and pulled him, right as the chasm reached him. "Move back!" I ordered.

He scrambled to his feet. "What do we do?!"

"The ship!" yelled Abigail.

I shook my head. "I'm not getting in that thing!"

The break in the earth grew stronger, sucking in the rocks nearest to us. "We don't have a choice!" shouted Abigail. "Get your stubborn ass in the ship!"

I didn't argue.

We piled into the triangle and the door closed itself, all on its own. Before I could strap myself in, the ship started moving, entering the tunnel before us.

I looked down at the controls on the front console. They were in another language, totally foreign. I was pretty sure I'd just traded one deathtrap for another.

We began rising through the tube, headed up. "Siggy, can you hear me? Freddie? Does anyone read me?"

No answer this time, not even static. Nothing.

The ship continued to climb the tube, riding what looked like a conveyer belt, pulling us higher and higher. We sat there for several minutes, and I wondered how far this thing went.

But then I felt the ship level and pause, totally stopping. I looked at Abigail, who was seated next to me in the front. "What the fuck is going on, Abby?"

She shook her head. "Why are you asking me?"

"You were the one who said to climb inside!"

"I didn't know what else to do."

"Both of you, look!" snapped Hitchens, pointing ahead of us.

A display appeared above us, imposed on the dash screen. It was a number, counting down from 10.

9...

8...

7...

6...

5...

"I don't like where this is going," said Abigail.

4...

3...

2...

"Shit," I muttered.

1...

The ship burst forward, suddenly moving. The momentum forced my head back in the headrest and I clutched the armrests, holding on for dear life.

The lights on the inside of the tunnel came faster and faster as we accelerated, eventually blending into a steady line of glowing blue lines. I expected us to slow down, but that never happened.

We just kept moving, going faster, all without any additional inertia.

Finally, right when I thought we might never escape this tube, another light blinked into existence, far ahead of us, and growing rapidly until we were right up on it.

We flew through the exit, exploding like a bullet from a barrel as we were sent towards the horizon. The walls around us ended and I saw the foggy atmosphere outside. The track beneath us exposed itself as we continued at an astonishing speed. Based on how far up we were, I guessed the tunnel had taken us at least eighty kilometers up, maybe more.

"Where are we going?" asked Lex, calm as ever.

Fuck if I know, I thought.

A sharp dip was just ahead. We dropped as we approached, then came up and into the sky, suddenly aiming towards—

"Look, there!" said Hitchens. "The Moon!"

It was coming into view now, the glowing blue lights of the orbiting goliath, so bright they dominated the sky.

As we drew closer, I could see trenches along the surface of the orb, lights shining from deep within. The chasms stretched across the rock like claw marks.

When we were close to it, I noticed one of the lights growing brighter than the rest. "Look at that," I said, pointing. "What do you think that—"

The light suddenly consumed us, covering the ship, and I felt a hard tug.

I banged the side of my helmet. "Siggy, talk to me!"

"Hold on!" shouted Abigail.

We turned into the light, heading directly toward one of the Moon's trenches.

"This must be some sort of magnetic beam," said Hitchens. "A grapple, perhaps."

"More like a fucking fish line," I snapped. "We've just been hooked!"

"It's taking us in," said Abigail. "Be ready!"

In moments, we dove into the chasm, entering the deeper recesses of this...well, I wasn't sure. Was it a moon? Was it even natural?

The metallic architecture along the walls seemed to suggest that all of this was artificial, but I'd never heard of anyone building something so big, not like this.

I noticed walkways all along the sides, sealed beneath a transparent, protective surface. Everywhere I looked, I saw pathways, each of them leading in different directions. Whatever this thing was, it was built to be traversed.

"Look there," said Hitchens, touching my shoulder. "It appears to be opening for us."

Sure enough, the wall ahead of us was splitting, its doors sliding apart to reveal some sort of landing pad.

The light around us dimmed as we began to slowly drift toward the deck, finally dissipating once our ship was firmly planted.

The deck was massive and well-lit, with several other ships sitting further down, identical to ours. "What the fuck is this?" I finally asked.

As if to answer, the door cracked, sliding down until it formed a set of stairs. Hitchens snapped back in his seat, surprised.

"Relax," said Abigail. "It's just opening. Lex, are you okay?"

Lex sat with her legs swinging back and forth, a soft smile on her face. "Uh-huh!"

Abigail squeezed the child's knee. "Good girl." She looked at me. "What now?"

Get ahold of Siggy and get the fuck out of here, I wanted to tell her. Run as fast as we can and don't look back. Blow this fucking rock to hell and then—

The dash lit up, without warning, and a woman's face appeared. She had white hair and blue eyes, with the look of someone in their mid-twenties.

"Welcome to *Titan*," she said.

TWENTY-THREE

I stared at the woman's face. "What...who the fuck?"

"I am the host of the Seed colony ship known as *Titan*. You may refer to me as Athena."

Abigail leaned closer to the dash, staring at the woman on the screen.

"Are you some kind of A.I.?" I asked.

"I am a true, independently functioning Cognitive."

"What does that mean?" I asked.

"If I may," interjected Hitchens. "I believe she is suggesting that she is a sentient A.I." He cleared his throat. "Or, rather, a self-aware intelligence."

"That is correct," said Athena.

"Can you tell us where we are?" I asked.

"*Titan*, a Seed colony ship currently in close orbit around a class-G planet."

I furrowed my brow. "What in the galaxy is a seed colony ship?"

"Please, exit the vehicle and all shall be explained." The screen went dark, instantly, and we heard her voice coming from outside the ship. "Awaiting your arrival, passengers."

This was crazy. We were inside some sort of megastructure, talking to a digitized woman. How many more surprises could I fit in a single day?

"I like her," said Lex from the backseat.

Abigail and I both turned to look at her. "You think she's nice?" asked the nun.

Lex nodded. "Can we go inside?"

"What do you think, Professor?" I asked Hitchens.

"We've come this far, Captain. It seems only natural to continue, though I suggest caution."

"No doubt about that," I muttered.

We each climbed out of the ship, one at a time. Hitchens held on to Lex while Abigail and I took out our weapons, ready for anything this place tried to throw at us.

"Your firearms will not be necessary," said the so-called cognitive.

Abigail looked up into the docking bay. "How do we know we can trust you?"

Athena's face appeared on the distant wall, a few dozen meters from the triangle ship. "Please, proceed this way so that I might explain."

I leaned in to Abby. "Keep your trigger finger ready."

She nodded, holding her rifle against her chest.

The four of us walked toward the rear of the bay, minding the other ships. By my count, there were half a dozen here. I wondered, briefly, if they were weaponized.

"This way," said Athena before disappearing from the screen.

To the right of where she'd been, I spotted an open corridor. Several pieces of the walls inside were detached, some of which had fallen to the floor. Behind the gaps, I spotted wires and circuitry, although it was beyond anything I'd ever seen. Nothing on *The Star* resembled this, except maybe in the vaguest of ways. On our way out, I'd have to steal a few pieces, just to see what they'd fetch me.

"Take the next left," said Athena's disembodied voice as we rounded the corner.

The door was closed, but slid open when we approached it. "Oh, my," said Hitchens. "Look at that."

It looked like a conference room, with a long table at the center. What stood out, and the reason Hitchens saw fit to make his exclamation, was the woman standing behind one of the seats, her hands clasped behind her waist. "Welcome. Please, have a seat."

We each stared at her. "What's this, now?" I asked. "I thought you were—"

"This is my hard-light representation," she explained, taking a few steps toward us. "There are emitters in certain areas of the ship which allow me to manifest my physical form so that I might interact with the animate world."

Lex let go of Hitchens and ran up to Athena.

Athena bent and smiled at her. "Hello, there."

"Hi, my name is Lex," said the little girl.

"Is that so?" asked the strange woman.

Seeing them together, I couldn't help but notice the similarities. Their hair and eyes were identical.

"You're pretty," said Lex.

"Thank you, Lex. You're very lovely, too," said Athena.

"This is getting creepy," I whispered to Abby.

"Jace, be quiet," she snapped.

"You don't think it's weird? Look at those two. They could be sisters."

"Stop being rude!"

Athena stood up, placing her hand on Lex's back. "Your Captain is correct," she said, looking at us. "Lex and I do share certain qualities."

"Y-You mean," stuttered Hitchens. "The two of you are...you're the same sort of...person?"

"Not at all," answered Athena. She glanced down at Lex, who was smiling, bright-eyed and cheerful. "She is an organic being, the same as you, but we do share a certain history together." She paused, touching the girl's helmet and, strangely, phased her hand through it, touching Lex's hand and running a finger through it. "We are remnants of what could have been."

"You're not making any sense," I said, reaching towards Lex

and taking her by the hand. I pulled her back to me and away from this woman, this cognitive. "Lex grew up far away from here. We didn't even know this place existed before today. How could you two be connected? How could any of this exist? Who the fuck are you, lady? What the hell is going on?"

A high-pitched noise hit me in the ear, hit all of us in the ear, making everyone cringe. It stopped suddenly, replaced by heavy static. I thought I could hear words, somewhere in it, like shouting in a snowstorm.

"Captain...read...ship...there!"

"Freddie?!" I shouted. "Fred, can you hear me?"

"I he...you...ome...in...!"

"Goddammit!" I shouted.

Athena held her hand up, like she was offering something, and then motioned gently to the wall beside me. "One moment, please. Your transmission is being disrupted by *Titan's* electromagnetic shield."

"Is there any way to clean it up?" I asked.

"I believe there is," said Athena.

"...aptain, do you read...? Please, respond!"

"Freddie, I'm here!" I answered. "You picking me up?"

"Yes, sir! Loud and clear! Please, tell me you know what's going on."

"Only kinda sorta, but don't worry. I think..." I glanced at Athena, who stared at me with a calm smile. "I'm pretty sure things are good."

"You don't sound very confident about that. Should I be worried?"

"Don't tell me how I sound, Freddie! Just get the ship parked and standby!"

Abigail snickered. "You really showed him."

"Don't test me right now, nun," I said, raising my eye.

Hitchens waddled closer to Athena. "Madam, if you wouldn't mind another inquiry."

"On the contrary," Athena assured him. "I do love conversations. It has been quite some time since I last had one with a human."

The Doctor nodded, smiling nervously. "Heavens, where to begin? I suppose the first question would have to be, is this ship, are you, from Earth? Is that how you came to be here?"

She smiled. "Oh, yes, Doctor. I was born there, as was this vessel. We are both made of Earth, though I must admit, it has been many centuries since I last looked upon it."

"Centuries?" asked Hitchens. "How old are you, exactly?"

"Exactly 2260 years have passed since I was born," Athena said.

I whistled. "Damn, Hitchens. You're not supposed to ask that."

"Might I ask, were you searching for Earth? Is that why you have come here?" asked Athena.

Abigail answered this time. "We've been following what we

thought was a map. Instead of taking us to Earth, it brought us here, to this system. Looks like we were wrong."

"On the contrary," said Athena. "Our meeting is imperative to your rediscovery of Earth. It is the reason I have allowed you access to this vessel."

"You knew we were looking for it?" I asked.

"Yes, Captain. In fact, it is why I brought you out of slipspace."

"That was you?" asked Abigail.

"Partially. I was only able to detect you because of the activation of a turn-key."

"A what?" I asked.

"Could you be referring to a small object, encased in a locked box?" asked Hitchens. "Lex was playing with one when we arrived."

"Your description is accurate," she said. "It is a communications device, although it has multiple functions. Upon its activation, and due to your proximity to *Titan*, I was able to detect you. Were you further away, our meeting may not have been possible."

Lex bobbed on her feet, excitedly. "I brought it! It's in my pocket!" She tried to remove her helmet, finally releasing the switch and undoing the seal.

"Hey, hold on a second kid!" I snapped, reaching for her.

She pulled away and dropped the helmet, letting it roll, then started for her sleeves. "Get it off," she said, tugging at the suit.

"Please," said Athena. "There is no need to be concerned. You are safe aboard this vessel. The atmosphere is fully functional and contained."

Lex managed to get her zipper down. "Ugh, why is it so hard?"

I looked at Abigail, who gave me an uncertain shrug. Hitchens did the same.

Fuck it, I thought, and turned my helmet, snapping it free of the seal.

I took a deep breath of the atmosphere. It was normal, although a little cleaner than *The Star's*. I had expected something thicker with age and decay, but it seemed this place was well-taken care of, even after all this time. "It's good," I finally said. "Kinda surprised."

"These types of facilities don't tend to get musky when they've been left alone for a while," explained Hitchens, removing his own helmet. "Space does a fine job of preserving them without much decay."

Lex found the artifact in her pockets, showing Athena with a happy grin on her face.

"I can't believe you've been carrying that around," I said.

"It's pretty," said Lex, as if that answered everything.

Athena took it, examining the device. "This appears to be fully functional. Many of the ships that left *Titan* took such devices with them, allowing those ships to stay in contact with each other across limited distances. I was surprised to see that you had two of them on your ship."

"Two?" asked Hitchens, looking at me.

"I may have kept the first one," I said, giving him a slight grin.

Athena smiled. "I must commend you for your forward thinking, Captain. Your acquisition of this device is what allowed me to track your movements. It is also how we can contact your ship."

"How's that?" I asked.

"One moment, please." She held the device and touched it to the nearby wall, causing the turn-key to glow. After a quick moment, Athena looked at me. "Now, speak and your associates will hear you."

"Speak?" I asked. "You want me to just talk to them? But they don't—"

"Captain?!" shouted Freddie in a terrified voice. "Is that you? Where are you?"

"Freddie? Can you hear me?" I asked.

"I sure can!" he exclaimed. "Where are you? Are you seeing that strange light coming from the surface? Did you do that?"

"Strange light? Did it start back up again?" asked Abigail.

"It has been reactivated," explained Athena. "The process is part of an energy transference procedure, necessary for *Titan's* nuclear power grid to reach full sustainability."

"You're siphoning power from the planet?" asked Abigail.

"The power grid on the surface was installed many centuries

ago. The system accumulated nuclear power and has been waiting for activation. Before now, I have been operating solely on reserve power."

"So, if I'm understanding you correctly," said Hitchens. "When Lex touched the tower, it activated the transfer from the generators below ground to this ship. Is that correct?"

"Approximately," answered Athena.

"Hey! Is anyone there? Whose voice is that? I hear a woman," said Freddie.

I leaned in close to the turn-key, which was still attached to the wall. "Sorry, Fred. We're inside the Moon, talking to a two-thousand-year-old woman about the secrets of the universe. Give me just a goddamn second."

"*A what*?!"

I was about to ask Athena another question when she froze, going completely still. The wall behind her flickered, showing a view of empty space above the planet. "Pardon me," she said. "It seems there are more ships arriving."

"More?" asked Abigail.

Athena turned toward the screen as six Sarkonian ships came out of partial-light speed.

"Is that who I think it is?" asked Abigail.

"You mean the psycho chick with the scar? Judging by the damage to the hull, I'd guess so," I said.

"Am I to understand that these individuals are hostile?" asked

Athena.

"Oh, yeah," I said.

Lex walked up to the screen, staring up at the Sarkonian ships as they grew closer to where *The Renegade Star* was floating. "Uh, oh," she said, looking up at me.

I placed a hand on her head. "You said it, kid."

TWENTY-FOUR

"Uh, hello?" said Freddie. "I think we have a problem!"

"Yeah, no shit, Fred! Siggy, are you hearing me?"

"Affirmative," answered Sigmond.

"Raise your shields and get your fat ass behind this Moon!"

"Doing so now, sir."

"Oh, dear," said Hitchens. "They must have followed us through the tunnel."

"Yes and no. Did you see how they showed up? It wasn't from a tunnel. They must have missed the break-off and kept going to the next S.G. Point," I explained. "Their engines must be better than I thought."

"*Titan* is not yet prepared for armed conflict," said Athena. "I do hope they restrain themselves."

"You can't fight back if they attack?" I asked.

"We lack the energy reserves to wage a proper assault. However, the shield is operating at 80% efficiency. It will hold off their attacks for quite some time, barring any unforeseen circumstances. However, such defensive measures will not last forever. *Titan* has its limits."

"We need to get *The Star* inside the shield," I said.

"Uh, Captain, one of the ships is signaling us," said Freddie.

"Siggy, can you put them through?" I asked.

"Yes, sir. Please hold."

There was a brief pause. "Captain Jace Hughes," said a determined, but familiar voice. "This is Commander Mercer Equestri. I have someone that would like to speak with you."

"What the hell is she talking about?" I muttered.

"He...Hello? Who is this?!" It was a girl's voice. She sounded almost delirious. "Th-They have my father! Please, someone—"

"Stop babbling!" snapped Mercer. "Tell them your name!"

"M-My name is C-Camilla. Please, someone help—"

"Did you hear that, Captain?" asked Mercer. "The girl, the same one you stole from Sarkonian space. She's here, not two meters away from me. Her father is with us, too."

"Goddammit," I said, talking through my teeth. "This fucking woman."

"What should we do?" asked Freddie.

"Keep her talking to you. Tell her I'm on my way to the bridge or something," I said.

"You—You want me to handle this?" he asked.

"Just do it, Fred! I need a second to think."

Dammit, I thought. I couldn't just turn myself over to this psychopath. People like Mercer always went back on their deals, even when they didn't need to. Not that I'd agree to her terms anyway. To Hell with that, but there had to be a way out of this. There was always a way, if you looked hard enough. I just needed to slow her down. I needed to...

"That's it!" I exclaimed. "Athena, how do those beams work, exactly? Can you grab onto bigger ships than the one we came here on?"

"It depends on the size of the vessel," she said.

"What about those?" I asked, nodding at the screen.

She froze again, just for a second, and then relaxed. "Yes, *Titan's* tractor beams can hold them, but not for an extended period of time."

"What are we talking here? How long?"

"Approximately ten minutes, based on current power levels."

Ten minutes. It wasn't much. Could we board their ship and rescue the girl and her dad while fending off a group of heavily-armed soldiers? Maybe, but it might be messy. "We'll need our gear and a ride out of here. Think you can arrange that?"

Athena nodded. "I can send you back to your vessel with the same craft you arrived in."

"Captain, you aren't suggesting we storm their ship?" asked Hitchens.

"We? No, just me and Abigail. The rest of you aren't trained for this."

"You expect the two of us to take on an entire crew of soldiers?" asked Abigail. "I'm certainly up for the challenge, but it does seem a bit suicidal."

"Might I make a suggestion?" asked Athena.

I shrugged. "Sure, what do you got, lady?"

"*Titan* still has an armory. Since you do not possess augmentations like Lex, you will not be able to fully utilize the weaponry. However, you may find some use from the personal shield technology."

"You have an armory?" I asked. "Why didn't you say so? Quick, show us what you have."

"Please, follow me."

"Hold on a sec," I said. "Siggy open the line so Mercer can hear me. Everyone else, shut up."

"The line is active, sir. Speak when ready."

"Mercer, if you're hearing me, this is Jace Hughes."

"Ah, Captain, there you are," she answered. "I'm glad to see my proposition spurred a response from you."

"Mercer, I'm sure we can figure out some kind of deal. You let those two go and maybe today doesn't have to be that bad. I'm willing to turn myself in. Just please, don't kill me."

"So, you've agreed to my terms? That's a wise move on your part. Move your ship out from behind that moon and prepare to be boarded."

"Give me ten minutes and you'll have yourself a deal. Do it, and I'll surrender."

"Ten minutes," she said. "But if you attempt to run or attack,

I'll order all of my ships to destroy yours. I don't care if we lose the child you're carrying. I'll kill all of you."

"I get it," I said. "Talk to you soon."

"Line disconnected," said Sigmond.

"Now," I said, turning to Athena. "Show me this so-called Armory."

* * *

The Armory was huge, with heavy lockers and cabinets along the walls. I tried to open the first one I saw, but it wouldn't budge. According to Athena, only a registered *Titan* resident could unlock them, and we certainly weren't that.

Athena touched my shoulder and a pale blue glow appeared, all along my body. It wasn't touching me, exactly. Just hovering over me, like a piece of clothing that sat about three centimeters from my body.

Then, it disappeared. "What just happened?" I asked.

"This is a personal shield augmentation. It has a set charge limit, currently of 35%."

"What does that mean?" I asked.

"The field will absorb projectiles, but please use caution. The equipment is not at full capacity and will only be able to withstand two or three attacks."

"That should be all we need," I said, looking at Abigail. Her body glowed as Athena activated the other shield. Like mine, it only lasted a second or two.

When we were ready, we made our way back to the docking bay, the same one we'd arrived at. Our triangular ship was still sitting there, only now it was turned around and facing the exit. Athena had said the flying process would be automatic, due to our inability to interface with the ship. I wasn't sure I understood the last part, but the rest seemed clear enough. *Keep your hands and arms inside the space jet at all times, kids, and let the crazy computer lady handle the controls.*

Before we boarded, I pulled Hitchens to the side. "I need you to stay here with Lex, Doc."

"Stay? Whatever for, Captain?"

"It's too dangerous, Hitch. You need to keep Lex safe. If the Sarkonians or the Union get their hands on her, she's going to wind up dead. This place—I don't know what the fuck it is or what to even make of it yet—but I can see it's safer than *The Star*, much as I hate to admit that."

"You make a good argument, Captain," he said. "I'll do as you ask. Just, please, don't get yourself killed."

I nodded, then joined Abigail in the ship. As the doors closed, I could hear Lex outside. She tugged on Hitchen's sleeve. "Where are they going? Why aren't they taking us?"

The doors sealed before I could hear the answer.

* * *

After we docked with *The Renegade Star*, Athena called the ship back to *Titan*, and I gave Freddie orders to move us out from behind the Moon.

"You understand the plan, right? You move the ship in, once Athena uses her beam on the Sarkonian ships. We target the lead, rescue Bolin and his daughter, then get the hell out of there."

Freddie nodded. "Right."

Abigail tossed him a rifle. "You'll need this if we fail and the Sarkonians try to take the ship."

He examined the gun, some uncertainty in his eyes. "O-Okay, thanks."

"You can handle it, Frederick," she said.

"Where's Octavia?" I asked. We were standing in the lounge, and I expected her to be there when Abigail and I showed up.

"She's with Alphonse," said Freddie. "He's doing better, but she had to replace the bandages."

"He's still out of it?"

"The trauma to his skull was pretty bad, from what she told me."

"Well, we can't worry about that now. Siggy, get ready to follow the plan I gave you."

"Yes, sir. I shall follow it with precision. Rest assured."

"Good man." I took a deep breath. "Everyone ready?"

Abigail raised her rifle. "Just give me the word."

"Athena," I said. "Do you hear me?"

"I do," said a disembodied voice. I was surprised at how loud it was, despite the turn-key being all the way in my room's closet. "Activating tractor beam in five seconds."

I looked at Abigail. "Let's go kill us some goddamn Sarkonians."

TWENTY-FIVE

The Renegade Star flew towards the squad of ships, taking aim at the centermost vessel, the flagship of this tiny fleet. "Fire when ready, Athena!" I barked, right as we were close enough away to use our weapons.

Several beams like the one that had brought us to *Titan* exploded from all across its surface, combining at a center focal point to create a massive ray of light. It swept across the void between us and struck the Sarkonian ships, consuming all of them at once.

Once it did, we were very nearly there. We had to do this quickly if we were going to make this work.

The timer had begun.

"Take us in, Siggy!" I ordered, not wasting a moment.

My ship approached the lead vessel, extending clamps and forcing a dock. "Overriding internal defense systems," said Sigmond. "The airlock will open in—"

The door slid open on both sides, with me holding my gun as two Sarkonians came running towards me. Both Abigail and I shot them instinctively, before they could even cross the threshold between our ships.

"—now," Sigmond finished.

"Yeah, thanks!" said Abigail.

"You ready?" I asked, unholstering a second pistol. It was the same one I'd taken from Spiketown.

She nodded. "Let's go get that family back."

We stormed through the airlock and entered the nearby corridor. A Sarkonian charged at Abigail, trying to take her by surprise, but all he got was the butt of a rifle and a broken nose. He fell backwards, against the wall, and Abigail shot him clean through the forehead.

I kept moving, knowing she was right behind. The second section was a corridor with multiple rooms, which meant multiple opportunities to be ambushed. We swept them, clearing the first four.

When we reached the fifth, Abigail grabbed my sleeve, holding me there. I gave her a confused look, but she motioned to the floor. There were two shadows, just beneath the door, breaking the light inside. I nodded, motioning for her to step back against the wall. She did, and I hit the switch to open it.

The idiot inside fired off his weapon as soon as the door moved.

Abigail and I were on both sides of the entrance with our backs to the wall. I curved my arm around and fired off a shot, right in his gut. As he started to fall, Abigail twisted around the wall and finished him with a headshot. Two and done.

We kept moving, arriving at the end of the hall. As we curved toward the center of the ship, down what I was sure would be the final climb, I was surprised by a group of three soldiers. They didn't hesitate to fire, and we didn't hesitate to dive out of the fucking way.

We hit the floor, sliding back into the previous corridor. I heard Athena's voice in my ear. "Shield reduced to 20%."

My leg had been struck and was glowing blue from the shot. There went one of my free hits.

Abigail leapt back on her feet and squatted next to the bend in the hall, holding her weapon low.

They had us pinned, which meant we'd have to either plow through them or give up and leave.

"Ideas?" she asked me.

"Only one," I said. "Time to make use of these shields."

She nodded.

"You go low; I'll go high. Stay close to the wall so you can take cover if you have to."

I peeked into the hall to see one soldier laying suppressing fire on us while the other two moved up along the corridor. One of them had a riot shield. They'd obviously come prepared.

Then again, so had we.

I dove out in front of the oncoming soldiers as they drew closer, firing into the first one before he saw me coming. I collided with him, grabbing his hand and pushing him into the one with the riot shield, which kept both of them from getting a clean shot at me.

Abigail fired from the corner, tagging the guy with the shield in his side multiple times. Her own shield flickered as the soldier at the end of the hall continued his suppressing fire on her.

"I'm out!" she yelled, diving behind the wall again.

I raised my pistol and pressed the barrel to the soldier's chin. He was still in my arms, trying to free his own weapon from my grip. No such luck. I fired straight into his skull, and a river of blood poured out of his nose as he collapsed in front of me.

The man with the riot shield had also fallen, just in front of me. I grabbed the ballistic shield and lifted it just in time to block the gunfire from down the hall.

I heard the voice tell me I only had 10% left. Apparently, I'd taken a shot without realizing it.

I pressed forward, holding the shield with my barrel peeking out the side. With one last bullet, I fired a shot at the third and final soldier. It struck him in the thigh and knocked him on his knee, where he struggled to get his rifle back up. Before he could, I reached in my side and, using my second pistol, sent the final blow to his forehead, exploding the back of his skull in the process. With confusion in his eyes, and the life in him gone, the soldier fell straight onto the floor with a hard thud.

I reloaded.

"Think we're almost there?" asked Abigail, wiping beads of sweat from her forehead.

"Don't know," I said, locking my magazine in place.

I helped Abigail to her feet. We double-timed it over the bodies and made our way into the centermost part of the ship, towards the bridge.

As we neared the door, a voice came on the speaker system. "Captain Hughes, stop what you are doing at once!"

It was Mercer, no doubt with some kind of ultimatum. Let her try and stop me.

"If you do not cease your actions, I will eliminate the two prisoners in my hold. Do you understand? This is your final warning!"

I touched the com in my ear. "Ready, Siggy?"

"On your command, sir," he answered.

I reached into my side pocket and retrieved a set of goggles, placing them over my forehead and flipping the switch. Abigail did the same. "Do it."

The doors slid open between us and every light across the ship instantly died. "Hack successful, sir," said Sigmond.

I slid the goggles over my eyes, and everything was bright again, only with a shade of green. "Let's do this."

Abigail and I turned into the corridor ahead of us. Several Sarkonians struggled to find their way in the darkened hall as we neared them, sniping each as soon as we had the chance.

The path led straight into the bridge, spacious and presently filled with panic. Someone was shouting. A woman I recognized. "Get the fucking lights back on! Tersa! Answer me you godforsaken A.I.!"

"I'm afraid Tersa is indisposed at the moment," said Sigmond, his voice coming over the speaker. "I am Sigmond, but my friends call me Siggy. You may call me Sigmond."

"Who the fuck is that?!"

We stayed low, moving fast. The woman yelling, the Commander with the scarred face, stood with her hand on a railing and a pistol in the other.

Not far from her position, I spotted Bolin and his daughter being held by two soldiers. I touched Abigail's shoulder and motioned towards them. She raised her finger to acknowledge and then went forward, coming up to them and raising her rifle.

She slammed the butt of the gun into the first man's cheek, cracking the bone, and in a fluid, quick movement, dug the barrel into the second soldier's stomach and fired. She did this in seconds. Neither of them knew what had happened until they were on the floor.

"Kill the prisoners!" shouted Mercer. She lifted her pistol in the dark, aiming it in Bolin and Camilla's direction. She couldn't see, but she fired anyway, hitting the wall behind them.

Camilla screamed, crouching on her knees and holding the sides of her head.

I ran towards Mercer, only to collide with one of her aides, knocking them down.

Mercer heard this and swung her barrel toward me, firing off a bullet. It hit my shoulder and the shield flickered. "0% remaining," Athena said.

Shit, I thought. *No more second chances.*

I reached for her weapon, grabbing the barrel right as she squeezed the trigger. The bullet fired off near my head, missing but giving me one hell of a fucking headache. My ears started ringing, but I didn't let myself slow down.

I knocked her hand against the railing, trying to force her to let go of the gun, while also burying my own into her waist. "Drop the fucking pistol!" I barked.

She struggled to move beneath me. "Let me go or I'll have your entire crew shot!"

"I wouldn't count on that, Commander!"

Abigail was with Bolin and Camilla, telling them to get up. She slid a third pair of goggles onto Bolin's forehead. "This will help," she said, activating them.

When he had them on, she told him to pick his daughter up and follow. I waited for the three of them to leave as I held Mercer back.

"I'm going to kill you, Hughes!" she snarled as she tried to move. "I'm going to kill every last one of you, starting with that freak girl you have!"

I nudged my goggles up with my shoulder, pushing them over my forehead. It was suddenly so dark, but I could still make out Mercer's face, only six or seven centimeters from me.

Without warning, the lights clicked on. "Control recovered," said a mechanical voice overhead.

I was suddenly face-to-face with Mercer. Her eyes filled with hate the moment she saw me. She opened her mouth to speak, no doubt to order her crew to kill me. I wouldn't give her the chance.

"Someone kill him!" she barked.

"Not today, you crazy bitch," I said, and then pressed my barrel further into her side and fired, watching her expression change from rage to shock as the bullet tore through her abdomen and out the other side.

She loosened her grip on the gun in her hand, and I snatched it away, tossing it behind me. Every eye in the room was on me as they reoriented themselves, finally aware of my position.

I swung her around and got behind her, wrapping my arm around her neck and buried the gun in her side, slowly backing away.

Half a dozen weapons were aimed at me in seconds, ready to blow me to pieces. I dragged Mercer back with me through the hall. "Watch yourselves!" I barked. "She'll live if you stay back!"

Mercer struggled under my arm. "Let...go!" she said, squirming. I felt blood, wet and warm, running out of her and onto my thigh. It was coming fast. She wouldn't last very long. I'd have to move.

I dragged Mercer down the hall while several of her subordinates followed me from a distance. They kept their rifles and pistols on me, but didn't fire. So long as I had their leader at gunpoint, I knew I was safe.

"Siggy, get ready to close the hatch," I muttered, right as I neared the turn in the corridor.

As I made the bend, still pulling Mercer, I felt her go limp. Her arms dangled on her sides.

"Sir," said Sigmond. "I must inform you, the woman in your possession has ceased her breathing."

"Damn," I muttered. The soldiers would keep coming, but I could run the rest of the way. I had a few seconds before they had me back in their line-of-sight. "Fuck it."

I dropped Mercer and started running. I heard the body hit the metal grate as I hurried through the hall. "Once I'm in, close the airlock!" I ordered. "Siggy, you hearing—"

I felt a sudden jerk in my shoulder, sending me against the wall. I hit the floor a few meters from the doorway, a numb pain filling my upper arm. I'd been shot before, so I knew exactly what was happening.

I turned to see a soldier aiming a rifle. *Fuck*, I thought, staring at the stranger who was about to end me. *I thought I was faster than that.*

Before he could pull the trigger, someone fired a shot off,

surprising both of us. It hit the wall behind the soldier, but before he could react, another one got him in the chest, followed by a third in the waist, and then a fourth in the neck. He fell to his knees and collapsed on his side.

I turned to see Freddie standing in the airlock, holding his rifle, breathing heavily. "Fred?" I said, not sure if I was hallucinating.

He reached out with his hand, grasping mine, and pulled me backwards while still aiming down the hall. "I've got you, Captain!"

I touched my arm, feeling the warm blood between my fingers. "Count me relieved to hear that," I muttered. "Now, let's get our asses out of here."

"Sounds like a plan to me, sir."

TWENTY-SIX

We arrived inside *Titan* and docked *The Renegade Star* in the bay. Before I could do anything, I heard Athena's voice come over the com. "Captain Hughes, please return to the observation room right away."

Abigail had taken the time to patch the wound on my shoulder during our short flight back to the Moon. It hurt like fucking hell, but I'd managed far worse before today.

Hitchens was standing outside, waiting for us when we arrived. He looked concerned when he saw the shoulder, but I gave him a dismissive wave. "It's nothing," I said, before he could ask.

Lex ran up to Abigail and gave her a hug. "Abby!"

Freddie followed, carrying Alphonse on one of the mobile transports. He was still unconscious, by the look of him.

Octavia rolled beside them. Since she and Freddie had still yet to come here, they couldn't help but gawk at the sheer size of the megastructure.

I took Hitchens by the arm. "Let's see what Athena wants."

"You want me to come with you?" he asked.

"Of course. You're the expert, Doc. Not me."

He nodded, and we started moving.

The doors to the small conference room slid open with Athena behind them, standing in the same spot she'd been before we left. "Welcome back," she said. "There is another ship inbound to our position. I need you to classify it so that I may assess the situation further."

"Classify it?" I asked.

She waved her hand at the back wall, changing it to show the Sarkonian ships, which were out of the tractor beam and firing on *Titan's* shield. "Here it comes," she said.

Right then, a massive ship appeared, nearly half the size of *Titan*. I recognized it as *The Galactic Dawn*.

Shit, I thought. "That's definitely hostile."

"I do not believe *Titan's* shield can withstand an attack by such an entity. We are still not at full power. I will be unable to return fire."

"What are we going to do, Captain?" asked Hitchens.

"We have to get out of here," I said. "Athena, how fast can this ship move? Can we outrun them?"

"*Titan* can only move at one-tenth the speed of light with its primary engines. The only viable solution would be to use slipspace."

"There's no slip tunnels in this system," I said.

The screen behind Athena showed The Galactic Dawn

dispersing its strike ships. "Tunnels?" asked Athena.

"Slip tunnels!" I answered. We were running out of time.

"Ah, you are referring to preexisting passages," said Athena. "Please, observe."

She froze in place, but only for a second, and the screen behind her changed, showing the section of space ahead of *Titan*.

A rift appeared, slicing through the empty void like a knife mark, revealing the inner green light of the slipstream. "A tunnel?" I asked, staring at it. "There was one here this whole time?"

"I don't quite understand," said Hitchens.

"It seems your people have forgotten a great many things in the time since your ancestors left my side, Jace Hughes," said the cognitive. "I can not only open existing slipstream tunnels; I can create them."

Titan pushed forward, though only a little, and suddenly we were there, inside the newly-created tunnel.

I looked at the other screen, which showed the area behind us. *The Galactic Dawn* was moving, too, no doubt trying to make its way inside the tunnel. Before it could, however, the rift closed, immersing us in the inner bands of slipspace.

I was stunned by what I was seeing. In all my time, traveling from one section of the galaxy to the next, I'd never seen a ship with the ability to create its own slip tunnels. "Be at ease," said Athena. "Your enemies will need to find another path if they hope to reach us."

"Where are you taking us now?" I asked.

"Not I," she corrected. "What follows is up to you." She looked behind me, and I turned to see Abigail and Freddie there, with Octavia in her chair. "To all of you," finished the cognitive.

Lex squeezed between them, forcing her way into the room. She walked up to me and took my hand. I smiled at her without knowing why.

I turned to Abigail. "We came here for a reason, didn't we? Might as well see this through to the end."

"That's right," she said, taking Lex's other hand. "We're not just going to walk away, not after everything we've been through."

"The path ahead will be difficult, despite all that you have accomplished," said Athena. "The journey is long. *Titan* is in need of repair and fuel. It will not be easy. Are you certain you wish to continue?"

I nodded. "Let's do what we set out to do." I looked at the ancient cognitive, at the woman from across the stars. "Athena," I finally said. "Set a course for Earth."

EPILOGUE

I stood inside a small room with Octavia. She had a needle in one hand, a pistol in the other.

If the man on the bed moved more than a few centimeters, she'd blow a hole straight through his brain. If he played nice, maybe I'd keep him alive.

After all, Alphonse had saved a little girl, not too long ago. He deserved to have the option of living.

The Constable cracked his eyes as he awoke, a dazed look on his face. He noticed Octavia's weapon first, then his eyes drifted to me. He was quick to assess his present situation, as I assumed he would be, so he didn't bother to ask what we were doing there with a gun pointed at him. Instead, he simply asked, "Where am I?"

I stood at the end of his bed, near his feet. "A lot of crazy shit has happened while you've been asleep."

He started to sit up, only for Octavia to raise her pistol. She gave him a look that suggested if he tried anything, things would get messy. He eyed the barrel, giving her a slow nod, then slid back down so he could look me in the eye.

"We'll get to all that later," I continued. "For now, it's time for the adults to have a conversation, just the three of us. Think you can handle it?"

He stared at me for what felt like a long time, his chest breathing steadily. I couldn't tell if he was scared or nervous. "What kind of conversation?" he finally asked.

"The kind where you tell me things," I answered. "The kind where I ask you questions, and if you say the right things, maybe you get to live."

Alphonse blinked his green eyes, taking a moment to process my request. With a long, quiet breath, he let out a gentle sigh. "Alright," he said at last. "What do you want to know?"

AUTHOR NOTES

A lot of crazy stuff happened while I was working on this book. First, I got sick and had to go see a doctor for the first time in three years. While I was recovering, Hurricane Irma struck Florida, devastating half the state with power outages, property damage, and flooding. It was a chaotic few months, to say the least.

Not that I let any of that stop me. I was in the middle of a book, after all, and I had to keep writing. The night of the hurricane, I charged my laptop and made sure I had a power adapter for my car, just in case. It was a good thing I did, too, because we lost electricity for about a week, and that initial laptop charge only lasted for five hours. Suffice it to say, I spent a decent amount of time in the backseat of my car, trying my best to get this book done on time. It was an interesting experience.

Still, I was one of the lucky ones. After the storm hit, my friend and I drove around town, looking at all the damage. Not only were several homes destroyed, but the flooding had wiped entire roads off the map, as rivers and lakes overflowed over the cement, collapsing it like paper, taking the neighboring homes with them. Even the bowling alley took a hit, burning to the ground seemingly overnight. If you want to see some pictures I took, check out my Instagram. I'd never seen anything so destructive, despite living in Florida for most of my life.

That aside, I loved writing this book. The exploration elements of science fiction have always been a fascination of mine, and I wanted to bring that curiosity into this series. As Jace and the gang continue their search for Earth, they'll keep discovering cool and interesting things like the launch loop, which they used to reach the moon.

So, what's next for our crew of misfits? Well, you can probably guess, based on the title of the third book, Renegade Moon. Our team will learn more about the mysteries of their new base of operations, its original inhabitants, and all the other questions that have been raised before now. We've already learned a great deal about this universe, but there is still so much more to discover. Lex's origins, for one, as well as the truth about how humanity lost contact with Earth. It's all going to be revealed soon enough.

Until then, keep flying, Renegades,

J.N. Chaney

ABOUT THE AUTHOR

J. N. Chaney has a Master's of Fine Arts in creative writing and fancies himself quite the Super Mario Bros. fan. When he isn't writing or gaming, you can find him online at www.jnchaney.com.

He migrates often but was last seen in Avon Park, Florida. Any sightings should be reported, as they are rare.

Renegade Atlas is his seventh novel.

Made in the USA
Middletown, DE
27 April 2018